BEAUTIFUL RAGE:
THE BREAK OF DAWN
Written By: Janaya Black
Copyright 2007
Photo By: Kevan Bowers
Cover By: Keith Roberts/KR Media
Edited By: Patricia Barthwell

Published By:
Black-Smith Enterprises
www.black-smithenterprises.com

Beautiful Rage: The Break of Dawn
© 2007 Janaya Black
All rights reserved

On the cover: Na'Keya model and actress

Published by Black-Smith Enterprises 2008

ISBN 10: 0-9762720-2-4
ISBN 13: 978-0-9762720-2-1

Printed in the United States of America

Acknowledgements:

Hello again,

Once again, I have to thank God for allowing me to finish yet another project. I thank Him for giving me the ability to use the gift of the written word to entertain all of you. This book was an emotional roller coaster for me, but I finally got it done!

I would like to dedicate this book to my grandfather, Hiram T. Smith, who has gone on to be with the Lord. I love you granddaddy, and you will always be in my heart. I miss you.

To my husband Rockey, I want to say thank you for always being my rock! Thank you for your continuous love, support, and encouragement. Without you all of this would be pointless.

Dre and MaKinlee, all of this is for you. Never be afraid to reach for the stars. Remove the words 'I can't' from your vocabulary. Never forget that you can do all things through Christ who strengthens you. I love you both very much.

To mom, dad, Bren, Butch, and all of my family and friends, thank you for your love and continued support! I love you all!

To my loyal readers, thank you for your continued support. To my new readers, welcome! I hope you'll stay with me for a while. Let me start your journey through this book by saying...hold on to your seat because you are you in for one heck of a ride!

Without further ado...enjoy!
Janaya

Beautiful Rage:
The Break of Dawn

Prologue

I remember a saying that I once heard my grandmother say, "time heals all wounds," and I have to admit that particular sentiment never sat well with me. Ideally, I suppose that it made perfect sense in the grand scheme of things, but even though the wounds heal the bearer of those wounds never forgets how they got there.

After my sister died, correction, after my sister was murdered at the hands of a deranged white man, I kept hearing my grandmother's voice in my head assuring me that time was going to heal my wounds. I tried to listen to Grandma, but eventually the darkness that was continually growing in my heart drowned her voice out- for good. It was at that point that I decided to do what I needed to do to help my own wounds mend.

It took me exactly three years, two weeks, and five days to pull it off, but I accomplished what I set out to do...I avenged the death of my sister. I methodically planned and executed the kidnapping, torture, and murder of her assailant. It was poetic justice to me, but the powers-that-be called it a crime. So, that's why I'm here in this God forsaken hellhole that many affectionately refer to as prison, waiting for the chance to tell my story to "The Voice"- that's what we call her in here.

"The Voice" is the reporter from the Women's Lib Magazine that previously told the stories of two other women and allowed their voices to be heard on the outside where people are so quick to judge. And now it's my turn. I killed a man and I have no regrets because he deserved it.

I want to be heard not because I feel the need to expunge my demons or clear my conscience, but because I just want the world to know that sometimes revenge is a sweet, sweet dish that is always best when its served cold.

Vanessa

"You know that you are the one to blame for all of this," I stated matter-of-factly to the headstone in front of me. It was a cool, balmy day and I wanted to do what I came to do and get out of there before the rain began.

It had been a little over two years, since I began my work at the Wayne County Women's Correctional Facility. My first assignment had been an interview with Marion Hayes, who was sentenced to life in prison for murdering her husband. She was the reason that I was here now. Her story was so compelling and heartbreaking that it moved me to use my position to help others hear the stories of incarcerated women. Not that I was trying to justify anything, but after hearing Marion's story, I just felt that people are often too quick to judge the actions of others based on the surface alone.

Once a month, I made it my business to visit her gravesite to clean off the tombstone I had purchased and deliver fresh flowers. For someone that had experienced so much ugliness in her life, it made me feel good to make her resting place look as though somebody cared that she was gone. It wasn't just for her, it was for me too because meeting her had changed my life. During our interview sessions I grew to respect her tremendously for her strength and resolve, so much so that I ended up considering her a friend.

It is because of her that I continued to push on with this assignment, or whatever you want to call it. My last interview was with a young girl named

Timberlynn Crawford, who got herself emotionally involved with a married man and ended up killing his wife. That case on top of Marion's death was so emotionally draining for me, that I actually thought about giving this up and going back to my former humdrum life of writing about politics. But then, I began receiving stacks and stacks of letters from inmates begging me to tell their stories so their minds could be put to rest. Thus, came the nickname, "The Voice", which is what they started calling me.

"I just don't know what to do with all of this," I admitted to the headstone, "I don't know how much longer I can listen to all of these people's stories and not go crazy. It's like I'm reliving these events each time they're told and it's really starting to get to me." I sat there staring blankly at the slab of stone as if I expected it to respond.

"This new case is a doozy," I went on, *"The next woman I'm supposed to go see killed her sister's accused murderer. If you could have seen the pictures of what she did to that guy… it would literally make you sick! I mean, what am I supposed to do with this? I don't know if I can keep doing this…"* I whispered.

"I just don't know if I can keep doing this," I reiterated to Yolanda, the editor and chief at the Women's Lib Magazine, in my office the next morning. She just sat and stared blankly at me as I continued to go on my tirade about why I couldn't continue the Prison Chronicles series.

"This is really starting to take a toll on me emotionally," I continued, pacing back and forth.

"Marion Hayes was already a difficult case for me to handle after what happened, Timberlynn Crawford's case had me dealing with repercussions from the victim's family on top of the emotional stress, and now this? Dawn Langston is obviously a nut-case."

"How do you know that?" Yolanda inquired.

"How do I know? Did you see what she did to that guy?" I asked disbelievingly, "How could someone do that to another human being and have no remorse? I watched the court video, that woman showed no emotion over what she did period. How do you expect me to go in there and try to make sense of this? At least with the other two stories, they showed regret and remorse for their crimes. That's how I was able to connect with them and tell their stories on a level where people might be able to identify with them, but this...I don't know what to do with this."

Yolanda said nothing as she gazed at me with a smirk on her face. After she was sure that I had finished my tantrum she stood up, handed me the dreaded Langston case file and said, "Look, I know that this is difficult for you, but do you remember why we started this series?"

"Yes, I do but..."

"But nothing, Jackson. We aren't doing these stories to justify the crimes that these women commit, we are doing these stories to give the public insight as to what drives these women to commit the crimes they commit. That's it. Do you know why I picked you?" she asked pointedly.

"No, actually, I don't know why you picked me. Please enlighten me," I replied sarcastically, as I sat down heavily and began to massage my temples.

"Because you have a heart and you wear it on your sleeve. That's what makes you such a great writer! It's your words that have given life to these women's stories because you were able to identify with them and feel what they felt! You didn't judge, you just told the stories and that's the whole point of the project- to just tell the story. Now if you want me to take you off the project, I will. I don't want to, but I will. Just remember this...you said yourself that 'you never know what a man's been through until you walk a mile in his shoes'. Now all I'm asking you to do is give this woman the same chance you gave the other two.

I know that her case seems pretty extreme to you, but if you judge her before you hear her story, aren't you doing the same thing that you condemned the public for doing when you started this project?" She asked in a way that clearly said that she really didn't need a response.

After that, I sat for a long while meditating on our conversation and decided that I would be a coward and a hypocrite if I didn't follow through with what I promised I would do. No matter how disturbing the prospect of this assignment seemed, I had to see it through or I would never forgive myself.

Chapter 1

Before I knew it, I was sitting in the prison parking lot, gripping my steering wheel so tight that my knuckles had turned white. "What am I doing?" I asked myself. Obviously, Yolanda's lecture had been more than effective, because once again I found myself sitting in the parking lot of that God forsaken facility, trying to summon enough courage to go in and do my job.

What was I afraid of? I honestly couldn't put my finger on what it was about this case that was making me so uneasy. Finally, I shook it off and forced myself out of the car. Somehow, I made my way into the haven of madness, where my newest prospect was awaiting my arrival.

"Hey, Bert," I said to the heavy-set security guard I had gotten to know on a first name basis.

"Ms. Jackson, you back again so soon? I think I'm going to have to make them give you an office up here pretty soon. You got a hell of a piece of work waitin' for you this time," she chuckled lightheartedly, as she checked me in. After completing the necessary procedures, she buzzed me in and led me down the long corridor to the visitor's chamber.

She paused before entering the combination to open the large metal door leading to the interview room. She looked at me with a serious look on her face. "Now don't be alarmed when you go in, Ms. Jackson," she warned, "we had to take special precautions with this one. She's prone to having extremely violent episodes from time to time, so her restraints are a little different from what you're used to seeing."

I nodded to acknowledge that I understood, then she finished entering the code and pushed the door open. I took a deep breath and forced myself to walk inside. There before me sat an extremely attractive petite woman, with a dark brown complexion, and a short cropped Afro. She was securely wrapped in a straight jacket and shackled to the table. The restraint contraption was wrapped so tightly around her body that all traces of femininity, outside of her face, were hidden within its confines. I tried to mask my shock by feigning a brief coughing episode, but her piercing eyes gazed unflinchingly, as she watched my every move.

Gingerly, I pulled myself together and sat down at the table. I was unaccustomed to the interviewee being in the room before me. Normally, I would have a chance to collect my thoughts and get situated before they arrived. Nevertheless, I was determined to remain in control of the situation and obtain my interview in the same fashion that I always had. Never mind the fact that the gruesome photos of her victim kept flashing through my mind every ten seconds, and now I was sitting across a table from her. My palms were sweating profusely.

The deafening silence was broken by the slam of the door as Bert returned to her station. The two male guards that remained in the room looked expectantly at me as if to say "get on with it already".

"Hello, Ms. Langston," I croaked, in a voice that I barely recognized, "my name is Vanessa Jackson. As you know, I'll be conducting the interview that you requested from the Women's Lib Magazine."

She smiled briefly and her eyes softened as she replied, "I know who you are Ms. Jackson, thank you for agreeing to meet with me. I'm sorry if my appearance startled you."

"Thank you. I have to admit that I wasn't expecting…this," I stated.

"Well, they seem to think that I am prone to violent episodes so this is the only way they would allow me to meet with you."

"Are you prone to violent episodes?"

"I am prone to violence only when violence is required. I believe that violence begets violence, Ms. Jackson. Are you familiar with the principle of an eye for an eye?" she asked pointedly.

"Yes," I admitted skeptically.

She sat back gingerly in her chair and looked me directly in the eye. "Do you believe in that principle?"

"I guess I believe in it in theory, but I also believe that no one has the right to take the law into their own hands."

"Is that what you feel I did?" she asked, with obvious amusement in her face.

"Yes, I do," I responded, holding her gaze defiantly.

"Well, Ms. Jackson, I really hope that by the time we finish this interview you'll be able to see it from my point of view. I don't expect you to condone what I did, but I feel that justice is in the eye of the beholder. Our legal system is set up to protect the rich and condemn the poor. People with money rule the world, and it was unfortunate for the man that killed my sister, that the decision of the United States justice system was overturned- by me.

"Contrary to popular belief, Ms. Jackson," she went on, "I am not crazy or insane. I planned that man's death down to the second, executed my plan flawlessly, and then I turned myself in. If I had to go back, I would do it again. Except, if I knew then what I know now, I probably wouldn't have turned myself in. Prison is not a fun place, but I am a woman of conviction and I accept the consequences of my actions. But make no mistake, I have no regrets about what I did."

As I sat there taking in the depth of what she'd just said, I realized that I had probably bitten off more than I could chew with this assignment. Then I thought of Marion Hayes and the promise I had made in honor of her to help these women tell their stories and be their "Voice". "God doesn't put more on you than what you can handle," I thought to myself.

I was scared to hear her story and I fully acknowledged that fact. I was afraid what hearing it might do to my character. After gathering every last bit of courage I could muster, I pressed the record button on my recorder, looked Dawn Langston straight in the eye and said, "Ready whenever you are."

Chapter 2

Ever since I was a little girl, I have always been obsessed with martial arts and the art of combat. So as soon as I was old enough to engage in physical combat, I took part in every form of martial arts my dad would enroll me in.

I loved every minute of it and I was good, very good. When I had a competition it was very seldom that anyone could beat me and if someone did it only happened once. I was meticulous about correcting the mistakes from my losses to ensure a flawless victory the next time I met up with that opponent. Our next battle would ultimately end with that person being mercilessly pummeled, due to my over zealous and competitive nature.

One thing I learned about myself was that I had an intense blood lust, and it was through that learning that I quickly realized I had to be disciplined enough to control all aspects of my temper. So as I progressed through martial arts training, I learned to harness the viciousness that resided within me, but it was through sparring and competition that I was able to release the animal lust I had for combat.

By the time I turned seventeen, I had become a second-degree black belt in karate. Though only a second-degree by official rank, I had the knowledge, tenacity, and viciousness of some fourth-degree black belts with only formalities hindering my advancement. Eventually it got to the point where I felt that I couldn't advance any further with karate, so I began to study the ancient art of Ninjitsu and pressure point control. I was vehemently obsessed with learning all the different ways of inflicting pain upon anyone who might decide to get on my bad side.

Carmen, my sister, thought I was a nutcase. We were only two years apart and she just couldn't understand why I would want to waste all of my free time fighting when I could be shopping. I didn't understand that either, but different as we were she was still my best friend. We did everything almost everything together when I wasn't training.

My sister was the most beautiful, kind, and sweetest person I ever knew. She would give anyone the shirt off her back if she thought they needed it. I can't tell you how many times she would make us late on various occasions because she would see a homeless person on the street and would just have to find the nearest fast food restaurant to supply a meal. There was never a time that I can remember that she wasn't doing something for someone else.

I remember when we were little, I always thought of Carmen as my very own little baby doll. I would always try to dress her up in my baby doll clothes and pretend like I was rescuing her from ninja, who were sent to kidnap her. When she was finally old enough to go to school with me, I would sneak out of my class everyday to go down to her classroom to check on her to make sure that she was happy and that nobody was picking on her. No matter how sneaky I thought I was being, somehow she could always sense my presence and would look up and wave at me. That was the bond we had; we always looked out for each other. If she was in a fight, I was in a fight, and if I was in a fight she was trying her best to be in a fight- even though she knew that I probably had everything under control and was enjoying every second of beating the crap out of whoever was stupid enough to actually pick a fight with me.

We grew up in a loving home with the best parents a kid could ever ask for. We never wanted for anything. My father made a great living as an electrical engineer, my mother worked for the city as a legal clerk, I was in my second year of college, and Carmen was a senior in high school on her way to college with a full academic scholarship. Our house was almost like the Waltons. My mother had dinner on the table promptly at 6pm every night and there was hell to pay if the whole family wasn't sitting in their assigned seats ready to eat when the last piece of silverware hit the table. Our dad spent most of his free time doting on Carmen and me showing us how ladies were supposed to be treated. From the time that we could walk, my daddy made sure we knew that we were his princesses, thereby raising our standards and expectations for the world and any future suitors who thought they might be brave enough to step through his door and ask permission to date one of his daughters. Yes, our lives were perfect until one day my sister didn't come home. I was twenty and she was eighteen.

Carmen was nothing if not responsible, so when my mother found her bed empty and untouched the morning after she had gone out to a birthday party with her friends, it was an immediate cause for alarm.

"Don't panic," I told my mom, "she probably decided to spend the night at Jasmine's house because it got late. She probably didn't want to wake anybody by calling the house phone. Just check the voicemail on your cell to see if she called." I heard myself saying the words, but even as they were spilling forth from my mouth, I didn't believe them myself. I knew my sister like the back of my hand and she would never stay out all night without calling our parents to let them know.

I had a nagging feeling in the pit of my stomach that something wasn't right. I didn't want my mother to worry, so I continued to falsely reassure her that the occurrence was surely a brain fart on Carmen's part and she would come bouncing through the door at any second. Slowly but surely the seconds turned to minutes and the minutes turned into hours, and still no word from Carmen.

By the time my father finally made it home, my mother was on the brink of hysteria and I was in a silent state of inner turmoil. While my parents contacted the police, I called all of Carmen's friends but none of them had heard from her since the night of the party. Jasmine said that she wasn't really feeling the vibe of the club so she decided to leave the party early to go home and get some rest. They said their goodbyes and that was it.

"Did anybody walk her to her car?" I yelled, vehemently into the phone.

Jasmine hesitated briefly and muttered a weak "no". I didn't wait for her to say another word before I slammed the phone down and tried to keep myself from throwing up. I knew right then and there that my little sister was in trouble. My mind urged and pleaded with me to be optimistic and think only good thoughts, but the realist in me knew much better. My heart knew without a shadow of a doubt that my sister was never coming home again.

Chapter 3

Three weeks went by before my sister's grossly mutilated body was found handcuffed to a bug infested bed in the filthy basement of an abandoned building in Detroit. A production crew scouting for movie locations happened to stumble upon the building and noticed a foul smell coming from the basement, and then the police were called.

When we got the call, we all decided that it was best my mother stay at home, being that she already had to be heavily sedated at regular intervals. We didn't think she would be the best candidate for the grim task of identifying the body, so my father and I went. On the way, I silently prayed and begged God to please spare us and let this all be some sort of horrible nightmare. The coroner tried his best to prepare us before he pulled out what remained of the body, but nothing he could have said would have prepared us for the horror of what had been done to Carmen.

As the sheet was pulled back to reveal what was once the most important person in my life, my father passed out. I just stood there staring mutely at the carcass that lay on the cold slab of metal in front of me. That was not my sister. My sister was beautiful with long, thick, glistening, black hair, brown eyes, full pouty lips, and a smile that could rival the sun.

The thing that lay before me was a misshapen form that had half its face caved in, two fingers missing from the right hand, bite marks on the breasts, bruises all over the upper torso, a chunk of skin bitten out of the inner thigh, and plugs of hair pulled out of her head. This could not be my sister.

"No," I said shaking my head back and forth, " this is not my sister! This can't be Carmen. There has to be some mistake..."

"I'm sorry, Ms. Langston, but we are very sure that this is your sister and we need for someone to positively ID the body so that we can proceed..."

"No!" I screamed, "That is not her! Now you get your people out there and keep looking for her!"

"Ms. Langston, please..."

By that time my ears had shut down and my mind went blank. The next thing I knew I was sitting in a chair outside in the hallway and a white police officer was kneeling in front of me, with a cup of water in his hand and a concerned look on his face.

"Here, Ms. Langston," he said softly, as he gently took my hand and wrapped it around the cup, "try to drink some of this." I feebly brought the cup to my lips and allowed the cold liquid to course its way down my throat. It seemed as though I could feel every molecule of water make its way through my body, slowly awakening my senses and bringing my back to the grim reality of where I was and why.

The officer sat down in front of me and waited patiently for me to catch his gaze before easing his way into asking the questions that needed to be addressed. "Ms. Langston, my name is Detective Christopher Jones. Are you alright?" he asked with genuine concern on his face. I gazed blankly into his face and said nothing as he continued, "Your father was able to positively ID the body for us…"

"So, now what?" I choked, fighting back tears.

"Now we find the person who did this," he replied softly, "I know this is hard for you and your family, but I have to ask you a few questions so that we can catch the perpetrator and get this thing laid to rest as soon as possible." I nodded my head absently.

"When was the last time you saw Carmen?"

"Friday morning, that was the third, I…we had breakfast together before I went to school."

"Where do you go to school?"

"Wayne State, the downtown campus."

"Did you come straight home after school?"

"No, because I had to go to work after class."

"Where do you work?"

"The Barnes & Noble bookstore on campus."

Endlessly he went on and on, asking me questions about my whereabouts, whether or not Carmen had a boyfriend, did she have any enemies that I could think of who would want to do her harm, did she do drugs, and was she in to anything out of the ordinary that we knew of. The more questions he asked, the angrier I felt myself become.

"Let me ask you some questions Detective," I shot back angrily, "do you have any leads yet? My sister was missing for three weeks! Three weeks! What exactly are you people doing, besides standing around scratching your heads, to actually solve this case?"

"Ms. Langston," he began calmly, "we are doing the best we can. Believe me when I say that we are going to find the person that did this, and that person is going to pay. Justice will be served."

Finally, after what seemed like hours, Detective Jones ended his barrage of questions and escorted me to the lobby where my father was waiting. His face was worn and heavy with fatigue, and his eyes were red and puffy from crying. I could tell that his heart was broken as he looked hopelessly at me and tried to manage a smile.

"Are you ok, baby?" he asked.

"I'm hanging in there, daddy," I replied, as I grabbed his hand and kissed it. "How are you holding up?"

"Well, baby, I wish I could tell you that I was doing ok, but I can't say that. I know that God has a purpose for everything that happens in life, but no parent is prepared to deal with the death of a child. I gotta believe that whoever did this to her will pay, I gotta believe that, but even so…it still won't bring my baby back." Then he broke down into heaving sobs.

As I stood there helplessly watching my daddy cry, my sorrow slowly began to evolve into anger. I could feel the blood in my veins begin to boil as flashes of Carmen's mutilated body flashed through my mind. I could almost feel her terror and pain as I imagined her begging her assailant to stop hurting her. What would make someone do something so horrible? My sister didn't deserve to die that way. How were we supposed to get through this?

"Come on, daddy," I whispered softly, as I gathered my father off the floor and helped him to the car. The drive home was a silent one. I stared straight ahead as I drove and daddy stared out the window, both of us thinking the exact same thing- how were we going to tell my mother?

Chapter 4

It took two weeks for the cops to arrest the primary suspect. Ross Stlyer, the name of the man who killed my sister. Ross Styler, Ross Styler...the name was embedded into my brain like a brand from a searing hot piece of metal. He was the brother of some big time drug dealer named Nico Styler, and thought he was untouchable. He was the kind of man that most women fell for with his dark good looks, fancy clothes, and jewelry. Aside from the fact that he was white, the thing that stuck out the most about him was that he had the darkest eyes I had ever seen. They were evil, piercing eyes that held no emotion. Even when they arrested him, he wore an air of cocky self-confidence that showed no signs of nervousness or remorse.

I had to give the task force behind Carmen's murder a lot of credit. Their hard work and long hours, all behind the ceaseless leadership of Detective Jones, gathered all the compelling evidence that lead to the capture and arrest of Ross Styler. Even though he was facing hard time, he always looked like he didn't have a care in the world.

It had been eight grueling months before Carmen's case was finally brought to trial, and my family was sitting on pins and needles. We sat through endless hours of questioning fired by the prosecuting and defense attorneys. Stlyer's brother hired the most crude high priced defense attorney he could find. The man showed no shame as he mercilessly tried to paint a vivid picture of Carmen as a drunken slut, who threw herself at Ross Styler in a frenzied state of passion, and then got herself kidnapped by some other nutcase she left the club with that night.

I could feel my nails puncture the flesh in the palm of my hand, as I stared at Ross Styler's face, while he watched his attorney with a look of pure amusement. As if he could feel my gaze boring into his flesh, he turned for a brief moment and looked me straight in the eye. As I held his gaze, he allowed a small smirk to pass his lips before he turned back towards the front.

"Did you see that?" I asked my mother angrily.

"Shhh. Dawn, please be quiet!" my mother admonished.

"Mom, did you see him just smile at me!" I yelled, causing the audience to turn and look.

"Order, order," the judge said harshly pounding her gavel. "Young lady, if you don't settle down, I will be forced to have you escorted out of here!" I bit my tongue and forced myself to sit back in my seat.

The case dragged on for three long weeks. The prosecution supplied mountains of compelling evidence that indicated beyond a shadow of a doubt in my mind that Styler was indeed the man that killed my sister. He was witnessed talking to her in the parking lot by a patron leaving the club that night, his skin was found under her nails, and one of his finger prints was found on the bat that was used to bash her skull in. Not only that, but it was also revealed that Styler had been brought up on rape charges twice before in the past, but both victims dropped charges. The only thing that left room to plant a seed of doubt in the juror's minds was the testimony of four people who boldly testified that Ross Styler was with them all night at the club, passed out drunkenly on a sofa in the back.

To me, this was an open and shut case. For the life of me, I could not understand why good taxpayer dollars were being wasted by bringing this case to trial, but nevertheless, I felt confident the jury would do the right thing and justice would prevail.

On the day of closing arguments, the prosecutor took the floor and delivered a closing argument that was filled with fire and passion. "Ladies and gentlemen of the jury," he began, "I ask you...no, I implore you to reflect upon the events that have taken place in this courtroom over the last few weeks. I know that this case has been a very disturbing and exhausting one, not to mention a huge interruption on all of your lives. But I ask you to consider all that you have seen and heard in this courtroom over the past three weeks.

Carmen Langston was a beautiful young woman, who had a very promising future, and was deeply loved and cared for by her family and friends. She could have been a doctor, a lawyer, or anything she wanted to be. She was an eighteen year old honor student who was looking forward to graduating from high school and going on to begin her life as an adult, until she met Ross Styler," he stated emphatically, pausing for effect. "When Carmen Langston met Ross Styler in the parking lot that night, she had no idea that this man would kidnap, rape, torture, and then kill her."

"Had she known that," he continued, " she would have run screaming away from him and gotten into her car and driven straight to the nearest police station. But...that is not what happened ladies and gentlemen. Please allow me to paint a vivid picture of how this entire scenario played out for you..."

"Objection, your honor!" shouted the defense attorney, "the prosecutor was not there on the night in question, so anything he would attest to is purely speculation!"

"Your honor, this is my closing argument and I am simply laying out the chain of events in the order that we believe they occurred as dictated by the coroner's report, the photographs, and witness testimonies."

"I will allow it, objection overruled," the judge conceded.

"But your honor..."

"I said I will allow it counselor!" she barked, banging her gavel impatiently. "Please continue."

From that point on, the prosecutor began to paint a vivid portrait of how Ross Styler sweet talked my sister into letting her guard down long enough for him to somehow force her into his car. Then he proceeded to take her to an abandoned building where he raped and tortured her for no less than five days. Then he went into detail about how plugs of her hair were violently torn from her scalp, two of her fingers were cut off, and pieces of flesh were bitten out of her skin.

With every gruesome depiction he replayed of the monstrosities that my baby sister had to endure at the hands of that lunatic, I felt my pulse grow louder in my ears. The sound was unbearable yet I couldn't move. I couldn't take my eyes off of him. The hatred that was festering inside of me began to creep into my throat in the form of fiery bile that threatened to expel itself. I fought the urge with every fiber of my being until I was able to calm myself with the quiet assurance that justice would prevail.

Even when Styler's attorney stood up to make his closing statement, I didn't fret because after the prosecutor's speech I knew that there was no way the jury would let that man walk out of that courtroom. When the judge dismissed the panel to reach their verdict, I took my mother's hand and led her out of the courtroom for the last time before our lives would be forever changed. On our way to the corridor, our eyes met again. For ten long seconds it was just me and Styler. I glared at him with every ounce of hatred I felt inside, but he only smiled and shook his head as he followed his attorney out of the courtroom. At that moment, I prayed and prayed hard for the Lord to please let justice be served.

Chapter 5

"We the jury find the defendant, Ross Styler...not guilty of murder in the first degree in the case of the state versus Ross Styler." Even as the waves of sound penetrated my ears and translated themselves into the audible words that we all dreaded to hear, my mind still couldn't process what my ears had just heard.

"What!" I screamed, jumping out of my seat. My mother buried her face in her hands while my father tried to restrain me.

"Dawn, please," he pleaded, his voice cracking.

"This is bullshit!" I screeched vehemently, as tears streamed down my face.

"Order, order," yelled the judge while simultaneously banging her gavel, "I want order in my courtroom this instant!"

I was past the point of coherent thought and reason. All I saw was rage, pure and unadulterated. Ross Styler was all smiles as he shook hands with his attorney and prepared to exit the courtroom a free man. Time seemed to move in slow motion as our eyes met yet again and he smiled back. Before he could turn away, I hurdled the partition and lunged at him with every intention of ending his life right then and there. But as luck would have it, my father, the bailiffs, and his attorney all managed to grab me before I could reach him.

"You bastard! I'll kill you! I swear I'll kill you! You won't get away with this, you son of a bitch!" I yelled, as my daddy and the guards dragged me out of the courtroom kicking and screaming.

The scene continued in the hallway until a strong pair of hands snatched me to attention and I was met with a pair of familiar blue eyes. "Stop it, Ms. Langston, or I will be forced to lock you up," warned Detective Jones. I looked around and saw how everyone was staring at me, and then finally my eyes fell upon my parents. My mother was sobbing uncontrollably while my father tried desperately to comfort her through his own tears. I immediately felt all of the fight drain out of my body.

"Do you hear me, Miss Langston?" he asked and I nodded yes. "Good. Now I am going to release you, but you have to promise me that you are going to behave yourself. Alright?" I nodded again and he let go of my arms.

I joined my parents and helped my father take my mother to the car. She was hysterical and my father was doing his best to hold it together for her and my sake. By the time we arrived at our house, there were cars lined up and down the street of friends and relatives who came by to offer their condolences.

I wanted nothing to do with any of it. I left my parents to go inside and deal with them while I stayed in the car staring blankly out the window. As I sat there my brain began to replay all of the events that took place over the past year from Carmen's death up until this point. I replayed all the evidence, all the testimonies, and most importantly the smug look on Styler's face when our eyes met for the first time.

The more I thought, the more the rage festered. The more the rage festered, the more violent my thoughts became until it was pure unabashed hate that I harbored in my heart. The face of my dead sister flashed before my eyes, as salty bitter tears streamed down my cheeks. Before long, the pressure that had been building within me erupted into a torrent of blood curdling screams that could be heard for miles.

The sounds that exploded from my body were filled with all the hurt, pain, and anguish I felt behind the loss of the one person in the world who shared the same blood as me. As I screamed, I began to beat on the dashboard, cracking the surface, then I jumped out of the car and wildly busted all of the windows with my bare hands. This rampage went on and on for I don't know how long, until my mother said my name and I immediately snapped back to reality. Everyone had come outside to see what all the commotion was about. When they saw what I had done, they all stood staring in a state of shock.

"Look at me," she said softly. "Look what you've done to your hands."

I looked down at my hands and my knuckles were bleeding profusely from the shards of broken glass, but I could feel nothing. My mother gently took my hands and kissed them softly. She led me into the house without giving anyone else a second glance.

As she knelt before me and cleaned my wounds she hummed softly to herself, as if to let me know that everything was going to be all right. I watched her as she calmly tended my wounds as she'd done so many other times in my life, and I wondered if our family would ever be same again. The inner turmoil I felt was wreaking havoc on me, so I couldn't imagine what my mother was going through because it was her child; flesh of her flesh. Parents were never supposed to have to endure the death of a child. That just wasn't the natural order of things.

While I continued to watch my mother nurse my wounds, I made my mind up then and there that this iniquity would not go unpunished. I decided that Ross Styler was going to pay for killing Carmen, and he was going to pay with his life. Come hell or high water, I was going to see that he suffered to his very last breath and there was absolutely nothing that anyone could do to stop me.

Chapter 6

Though life went on, it seemed as though my family never could quite put the pieces back together. Carmen's absence left a huge chasm in our family unit and we couldn't figure out how to patch it up. My mother and father seemed to age considerably. Their youthful, happy dispositions had been replaced by depressed listlessness. My mother took to pill popping to get through the days without breaking down and my father lost his zest and cheerful demeanor. They both seemed to merely go through the motions of imitating life as they knew it.

Me, on the other hand, I was focused on my agenda. I decided to quit school and get a job so that I could fund my revenge operation. I told my parents that I just needed some time to get back into the mind frame of going to school. They weren't happy about it, but ultimately conceded that I had to do what I thought was best. Deep down they knew that they wouldn't be able to change my mind, so they decided to let that battle go. Little by little I was taking small strides toward saving all the money I could so that I could do what I needed to do to get a place of my own.

From that point forward, I began to plan and train harder than ever. For what I was preparing to do my mind, body, and spirit had to be focused and totally in sync. I was in the gym working out and sparring six days a week. I only took off one day a week, and that day was used solely for the purpose of scouting locations to carry out my plan.

The days went on and the days turned into weeks, the weeks into months, and before we knew it, a year had passed since Carmen was killed. I was relentless in my drive to be flawless in my execution. I had primed my body to be a weapon. My hands were faster, I was physically stronger, I had mastered every pressure point tactic I could find, and my hatred for Styler burned just as strong as ever.

After six months of working, I had finally saved up enough money to rent an apartment. I decided to move out to Inkster, a small suburb outside of the city, because I didn't know anyone out there and nobody knew me. I wanted to be as low on the radar as possible. My parents did everything they could to convince me to stay home, but I assured them that I would be ok. "It's time for me to get out on my own," I explained, kissing my mother.

"Ok, baby," she said, trying not to let the newly formed tears in her eyes fall.

Once I settled into my apartment, I purchased only the bare necessities. There was no need to decorate and make the place all homey because after what I was planning to do, I was sure that I wouldn't be coming back. That realization was enough to make me sit down and evaluate the magnitude of what I was planning; to kill a man in cold blood. What would I do after that? I knew I would have to disappear. What would that do to my parents? It would almost be like they were losing another child, since I didn't know if I would ever see them again. And what if I was caught? Could I spend the rest of my life in prison?

Oddly enough, none of the realistic answers to any of those questions was enough to turn me away from my course of action. I resolved to continue as planned. With the apartment out of the way, I was free to come and go as I chose without having to worry about making up excuses to my parents about what I was doing. While staying at home rent free, I had saved enough money so that I wouldn't have to worry about finances. I could take off work and still afford to buy everything I needed to carry out my plans.

After I had everything in place with my personal situation, it was time to find a hideout where I could carry out Ross Styler's death sentence with no interruptions. After three weeks of patiently searching every remote location I could think of, I stumbled upon an abandoned farmhouse on the outskirts of Romulus. It was perfect. It was on a few acres of deserted land, the grass was over grown and unkept, and the house itself was boarded up.

I waited until dusk one evening to venture onto the property for a closer look. As I approached the structure, I noticed that it had a haunted look about it with its raggedy unwelcoming porch, flanked with wood-rotted steps. The boards on the windows barely protected the glass behind that showcased holes the size of baseballs.

I leaned on the door slightly to see if it would give way, but it did not budge; that was a good sign. I hurried around to the back to see what other entrance might be available. To my delight there was a basement entrance that regressed down a small flight of stairs. I quickly walked down the stairs to test the door and found that it was also locked, but not as sturdy as the front door. One swift kick and the house was an open book.

Drifting in slowly, I switched on my flashlight and gave the room a quick sweep. At first glance, it appeared to be a typical basement only it was infested with spider nests, and Lord only knew what other types of vermin. After making a full assessment of the basement, I crept up the stairs to see what else the house had to offer. Once upstairs I ventured into the kitchen, which for the most part was still in pretty good shape. The living room and dining room were both large rooms that showcased dusty hardwood floors with empty light fixtures hanging from the ceiling. To the left of the basement stairs in the kitchen was another staircase that went up to what I could only assume were bedrooms.

After completing my investigation of the second floor, I stood silently in the center of the room just listening to the house to see what telltale sounds might whisper to me in the darkness. I wasn't afraid, I actually felt a sense of calmness settle over me. This place was perfect.

I could feel my heart rate increase at the mere thought of inflicting revenge upon the man that had torn my family apart. There was a lot of work to be done, but my hatred fueled me. I could set up shop here, carry out what I needed to do, and no one would ever know.

Chapter 7

After affirming my decision to set up shop in the vacant farmhouse, I began executing my shopping list. My days were spent picking up various supplies and gadgets to get the house ready for Styler's arrival. In addition to that, I also made special enhancements to my car to accommodate his transport to my hideout and I have to say that my fighting skills were at their peak. Between working, training, and sneaking to the farm to set up shop, I barely managed to find time to feed myself. I was a woman obsessed.

"Dawn, I swear if you loose any more weight, you are going to disappear," my mother chastised.

"I'm ok, mom," I assured her, "I've just been really busy that's all."

"Well, you need to come by more often so I can make sure you're eating right. Your father is worried about you."

"I'm fine," I insisted. But as the days wore on, I became more and more consumed with getting everything in order. I didn't need food; my lust for vengeance was the only nourishment I needed to get me through the day.

After six months, I had completely gutted out the farmhouse basement and converted it into a makeshift hideout. I purchased a generator to provide the energy needed to carry out various tasks in getting the basement set up to my specifications. In my tenacious drive to be meticulous in my planning, I acquired a means of getting the not so legal utensils that I would need in the days to come.

Now that the space was ready, I could focus all of my free time on Styler. I began to follow him so that I could clock his every move and learn his habits. Every morning before work, I was up at five a.m. sharp so that I could trail him until it was time to go to work at nine. After work, I would pick right back up where I left off until it was time to train.

Before long, it got to the point where I could get so close to him that he couldn't fart without me being able to smell the stench. And the best part of it all was that he was so careless and cocky in his actions that he never even noticed that I was there. I was able to blend into the shadow like an angel of death counting down the seconds for Styler's life to end.

I witnessed countless drug transactions and assaults. He was as ruthless as he was cocky. I even saw him take a man out in the alley behind a club and beat him unconscious with the butt of his gun because he brought him the wrong drink. Another time, I saw him force a woman to perform fellatio on him while holding a gun to her head. For the life of me, I couldn't understand how this man was able to continuously get away with doing the things he did. Each injustice I witnessed made my lust for his suffering that much more all-consuming.

I even went as far as to leave a picture of Carmen on the windshield of his car one night just to see what his reaction would be. It was gratifying to see that he was visibly shaken when he saw it. He looked around angrily trying to see if he could catch a glimpse of who would have had the gumption to do something so callous. Then to my surprise he did something totally unexpected.

"You think you can scare me?" he yelled into the night. "You think I don't know you've been following me? Watching me?"

I slumped down in the seat of my car gripping the steering wheel so hard my knuckles turned white. "How does he know?" I asked myself, "Did he see me?" I was starting to panic, but then I forced myself to breathe evenly so my heart would stop racing. Once I felt the panic subside, I opened my eyes and focused on Styler who was still standing outside his car staring into the dark.

"I know you've been following me, Detective Jones! You don't scare me, and if you keep harassing me, I'm going to haul your ass back to court!" he shouted. "Do you hear me?"

A wave of relief swept over me as I smiled to myself. He thought that Detective Jones was following him. But wait a minute! If he thought Detective Jones was following him, then maybe I wasn't being as careful as I thought I was. Or even worse, maybe Detective Jones was watching him and I had missed it in my homicidal obsession.

My thoughts went into overdrive, as I tried to think back and remember if I had witnessed anything out of the ordinary during my stakeouts. I couldn't think of anything. Slinking up slightly in my seat, I quickly surveyed the street to see if I could see any other vehicles that could appear to be on stakeout and saw nothing.

"That's ok," Styler said laughing to himself, "I know you're out there. You pigs won't ever get nothing on me." With that, he crumpled up Carmen's photo, threw it on the ground, got into his car, and peeled out.

After he was gone, I sat there for a long while contemplating what my next move should be. I'd come too far to let anything get in the way of my revenge, but if that cop was in the picture then that meant that I was going to have to be a lot more careful. Ultimately, his involvement was of no consequence because nothing short of death or imprisonment was going to stop me from sending Ross Styler straight to hell where he belonged.

Chapter 8

The very next day I decided to pay Detective Jones a visit. I had to find out if there was any truth to Styler's rantings before I made any more moves. So, I picked up a cookie bouquet and presented myself unannounced at his office to offer my sincere gratitude for all of the hard work he had done on Carmen's case.

"Well hello, Ms. Langston," said Detective Jones, as he made his way to the front lobby where I was seated. "This is an unexpected visit. What can I do for you today?"

He extended his hand for me to shake, and I stood to present him with the cookie bouquet I had purchased. His blue eyes lit up with amusement as he turned the package around examining its contents. As I stood there, I couldn't help but notice how handsome he was with his closely faded hair, piercing blue eyes, and perfectly trimmed goatee. I mean, I remembered him being a nice looking guy the first time I met him but under the circumstances, I was in no mood to flirt. But now as I sized up what may have turned out to be my biggest obstacle in this whole situation, I couldn't help but feel an involuntary attraction to him.

"What's this?" he asked innocently.

"I just wanted to stop by and give that to you as a token of appreciation from me and my family for all of the hard work that you did on my sister's case."

"Thank you, Ms. Langston," he said appreciatively, "it means a lot that you would think to do something like that, but I was just doing my job.

Unfortunately, even though we do the best we can, things don't always work out the way they're supposed to."

There was an awkward silence as we stood there staring intently at each other and then he said, "Would you like to come in to my office for a moment?"

"Yes, that would be great," I responded quickly.

As I followed him, I quickly tried to formulate a plan as to how I was going to get him to talk to me about Styler without giving myself away. I knew that cops were suspicious by nature, but due to the fact that Carmen was my sister, I didn't think that it would be too hard to get him to open up. I just had to remember not to say too much.

"Please have a seat," he offered, motioning me to a hard wooden chair in front of his desk. "So tell me, how have you been?"

"I have my good days in the midst of all the bad ones," I admitted.

"I see. How have your parents been holding up?"

"They're doing as well as they can. We really don't talk about it much. I guess that's their way of dealing with it. So that kind of leaves me on my own. I still have a lot of unanswered questions."

"Like what?" he asked.

"Like how does a man get off on a case like that when there was so much compelling evidence against him? I mean, I still lose sleep at night wondering how it all went down. It just doesn't seem right."

"Well Ms. Langston…"

"Please call me Dawn."

"Ok, Dawn," he began, "sometimes the justice system doesn't always work the way that we think it should. When you put things in the hands of people, they always have the potential to be flawed because people are flawed. But as a law enforcement official, I have to look at the big picture and believe that things will work out for the greater good so that I can continue to do my job everyday. I can't explain what happened in that courtroom because I really don't understand myself why people lie for individuals like Ross Stlyer, but our law says that everyone is innocent until proven guilty and that's what we have to abide by. I know that doesn't make you feel any better, but I really don't know what else I can say."

"I understand," I said, "but I just wanted you to know that my family and I know how hard you worked getting all that evidence, so I just wanted to stop by and give you a little token of our appreciation."

"I do appreciate it," he said smiling.

I glanced around the office and noticed that he didn't have any family photos anywhere to indicate whether or not he was married, then I allowed my eyes to pass briefly over his left hand and saw that there was no wedding ring either. With no ties at home he would certainly be free to trail a suspect at his leisure, so I decided to press a little more.

"Do you know if Styler is still here in Michigan? I would hate to think that he's still prowling around here looking for some other young girl to prey on."

"He's still here, but rest assured we're keeping a very close eye on him," he stated with a hard look in his eye, "me personally, I have taken a special interest in making sure that Styler is on his best behavior."

I looked down and smiled to myself. So, he had been following him around. It made me feel good to know that someone else cared about what happened to my sister. But I shook it off and reminded myself why I was there. If this man ever found out about what I was planning to do, then I would become the focus of his attention. I couldn't allow that to happen under any circumstances.

"It's good to know that someone besides us cares about what happened to my sister," I said finally looking him straight in the eye. "Thank you again, Detective Jones."

"Please, call me Chris. And if you ever feel the need to ask anymore questions or you just want to talk, please feel free to call me," he said, handing me one of his business cards. "I'm not just saying that, I mean it. Call me if you need me…for anything."

"I'll remember that," I said, as I took the card and stuck it into my purse. "Ok then, Detective…I mean Chris, I think I have taken up enough of your time. Thank you again and enjoy those cookies."

"I will Ms. Langston," he replied, " and you take care of yourself."

Once I was safely within the confines of my car, I breathed a heavy sigh of relief. He had no idea that I had been following Styler, and now that I knew for sure about his involvement, I was going to have to be a lot

more careful about my daily activities that surrounded
him.

I felt much better now that I knew what I was
dealing with, because the hour of truth was quickly
coming upon me. Because Jones or no Jones, Styler was
going to die.

Chapter 9

Three years, two weeks, and five days after the death of my sister, I woke up on the day that was to be the first day of the rest of my life. As my eyes adjusted to the darkness that surrounded me, I focused in on the clock next to my bed and the time was four-thirty five a.m.

As I lay there, all the events of the past three years replayed themselves in my head for the millionth time. I saw Carmen's face as we laughed together, then I saw her mutilated corpse laying on the cold slab of steel in a drawer at the morgue. The faces of my parents flashed before me as they held each other sobbing at my sister's funeral, then I saw the casket being lowered into the ground. Finally, I saw the smiling face of Ross Styler looking smugly at me after the jury declared him innocent on all counts of my sister's murder.

My eyes glazed over as I continued to stare at the ceiling, trying to force the tears away. There would be no more room for emotion in my life from this point on. I had trained myself to think and act like a machine. I was preparing to take the life of another human being. Not only was I preparing myself to take his life, but I was going to torture him every step of the way. I wanted him to experience all the pain and suffering he had inflicted upon my sister and I wanted to hear him beg for mercy. Once I began this journey there would be no turning back.

I had to admit that the thought of no turning back weighed heavily on my heart. My parents had brought us up in a God fearing home. Even in my blind rage and intent to seek revenge, part of me cried out to turn away from my wrath, which would surely lead me down the path of self-destruction. The inner turmoil I faced was enough to drive me to my knees for the first time in three years, to seek guidance from God. I knew that what I was going to do was wrong, and I also knew that all I had to do was turn away from my present course of action and walk away. Just walk away. Kneeling next to my bed, I prayed to God with hot salty tears streaming down my cheeks. I didn't pray that He would give me the strength to turn the other cheek, but rather I prayed that once it was over he would find it in his heart to forgive me. I was going to do it my way first and ask for forgiveness later. I had tried to do things the right way the first time around and it didn't work out, so I hoped that He would understand.

With dry eyes and a made up mind, I stood to my feet and looked at myself in the mirror. It was time to put the plan that I had meticulously agonized over for so long, in to motion. Today was the day that Ross Styler and I would meet again.

Chapter 10

"Time's up," the security guard stated.   I abruptly snapped out of the trance like state I had fallen in to while listening to Dawn's story. I pushed the stop button on my recorder and allowed myself to meet her gaze. We stared unflinchingly at one another for a few long seconds. Then I began to gather my belongings in an effort to appear more in control of the situation than what I actually was.

"Well, Ms. Langston, it looks like we'll have to pick this back up next week," I said, trying to sound nonchalant.

"Ok," she replied, maintaining her intense gaze. I continued to pack up my things all the while making it seem much more tedious than it really was. I didn't want to have to look at her again while the guard prepared to transport her back to her cell.

Without making any effort to end our session with pleasantries, I threw my bag over my shoulder and made a beeline for the door. The guard couldn't get it open fast enough, and I was out of there like a bat out of hell.

Once I was safely behind the wheel of my car, I sat for a moment and tried to figure out why I was so freaked out by this woman's case. I had seen her and she wasn't a monster. She seemed to be in possession of all her faculties, yet I was honestly dreading to hear the rest of this story.

Since she had given me the gruesome details of her sister's murder, I headed over to my office to request the case file and photos from Carmen Langston's case. I wanted to review the details more thoroughly before our next visit. When I took on Dawn's story, up until that point, I had only focused on what she had done to Ross Styler.

After I finally made it home, I immediately turned on some music, ran myself a bubble bath, and fixed myself a glass of Merlot to calm my nerves. As the lavender chamomile filled my nostrils with its intoxicating scent and Babyface sang about the whip appeal that some nameless woman was putting on him, I slowly felt my body begin to relax. The soothing tendrils of the Merlot coursed its way through my system, warming me from the inside out as I allowed myself to drift into my thoughts.

"What the hell is wrong with me," I wondered out loud, "I am Vanessa Jackson, one of the best journalists in the city and I am letting a story get the best of me. I have got to pull myself together."

When I replayed the events of the day in my head, I kept seeing the face of Dawn Langston as she calmly recounted the events of her life. She obviously loved her sister very much, but that wasn't the thing that was bothering me. In the grand scheme of things, there had been hundreds if not thousands of cases of gang related violence where people were killed by acts of revenge.

What was really scaring me was the thought that after it was all said and done, I might end up identifying with this woman in some way and lose my faith in the justice system. As a journalist, I had to remain objective and neutral. I couldn't go around condoning violence on any level. But by the same token, I had a mother that I was very close to and I couldn't imagine where my thoughts would turn if someone did to her what had been done to Carmen Langston.

What if after this story was over, I lost my ability to remain objective through it all? I was just supposed to be the "voice" and tell the stories, so that the world would know that everything isn't black and white like the media tries to portray it. There are always three sides to every story; the right side, the left side, and the truth that lies somewhere in the middle, and all I wanted to do was give the left side a chance to be heard. But in my crusade to be the champion of the underdogs, I was getting way more than I bargained for.

I was beginning to question my sense of morality because I found myself empathizing with these women. With Marion Hayes, I felt every word she spoke to the depths of my heart. I had never been through nearly as much as she had in my sheltered life as an only child of two prosperous loving parents, but I could see the pain in her eyes and I could feel her sense of loss and remorse. With Timberlynn Crawford, I completely identified with her, because I too had loved a man that I had given my all to and he cheated on me. Though he wasn't married and I did not fault the woman involved, thoughts of violence did enter my head when I discovered his infidelity after giving him three years of my life. I could never see myself doing harm to another human being, but just to know that I had thought about it was enough for me to question myself.

Could I ever take the life of another human being? Before taking on this project the answer would have always been no. Never under any circumstances could I or would I ever do anything to hurt someone else. But after talking to these women and hearing about their lives and the circumstances that drove them to extreme acts of violence, I had to wonder if I too could be driven to do the unimaginable.

I knew then that what was scaring me the most was the fact that after I completed this assignment I would get my answer and it might be one that I wasn't prepared to deal with.

By the time my next appointment with Dawn rolled around, I was determined to get my act together. This was no different from any other assignment I had taken on, and I reiterated that to myself over and over again. I had thoroughly reviewed the case file for Carmen Langston, so at that point I felt I was more prepared to approach the situation from a more informed standpoint. It also allowed me to grasp a bigger hold on Dawn's frame of mind when she saw the body of her sister for the first time. I felt that I had reviewed this case from every possible angle and I was prepared.

Drumming my fingers absentmindedly on the table as I waited for Dawn to be escorted in, the ticks from the clock on the wall seemed to keep cadence with my thoughts. After counting each tick over and over again for what seemed like an eternity, the guards finally brought her in and secured her restraints.

Oddly enough, she didn't look as alarming as she did the first day we met. Her countenance was more relaxed, as she adjusted herself to face me more comfortably.

"How are you today, Ms. Langston?"

"I'm doing alright, all things considered," she responded lightly.

"Great. So, if my memory serves me correctly," I began, as I pushed the record button on my recorder, "when we left off, you were getting ready to tell me about the day you put your plan into action."

Staring blankly off into space with a slight smirk on her lips she replied, "Yeah, like I said... it was the first day of the rest of my life..."

Chapter 11

That Monday morning after I left my house, I went to Styler's house as usual. The only difference was that this time I would not be cutting out at eight-thirty to go to work. I had taken the week off so that he and I wouldn't be interrupted during all the special activities I had planned.

Like clockwork, Styler came out of his house promptly at seven o'clock. As usual, he was impeccably dressed in a linen Versace pants suit that was tailor made especially for him. I watched ruefully as he admired his reflection in the tinted window of his car and stroked the perfectly trimmed goatee on his face. As expected, he jumped into his Benz and peeled off to meet up with his brother at Big Boy for breakfast, over which they would discuss all their criminal activities for the day. It really amused me to know that they ran their shop just like a real business with real work hours and everything.

After breakfast, he would be heading over to the club to drop off drugs for his flunkies and pick up the cash and receipts from the previous night because his brother didn't trust anyone else to handle his money. From there, he would usually make a run to the bank to make the deposit before heading back home to smoke something. Then he would go back to sleep until regular people got off work. Only today he wouldn't make it to the bank.

While I sat waiting outside the club parked in the alley about fifty feet from the side door where Styler would exit, I looked in my rearview mirror to admire my disguise. I had covered my own long hair with a long black wig with Chinese-styled bangs that accentuated my face, and my make-up had been flawlessly applied to bring out the best of my features to make me look inviting, yet not too available. The piece de resistance to my whole facade was the green contact lenses I had placed in my eyes.

I had also purchased a brand new outfit for the occasion. Special order for Styler, I purchased a skin-tight black leather mini skirt that barely covered my ass with a flaming red Dolce & Gabana satin top to match. The skinny black six-inch Prada heels I was wearing completed the look I hoped screamed "hooker" with a sense of style, which was the type that I'd seen Styler take back to his house on more than one occasion.

After Styler walked into the club, I popped my hood, jumped out of the car, and ran around to the front of the vehicle. After propping the hood up, I looked around to see if anyone was watching while I pretended to fiddle around. Satisfied that I wasn't being watched and that no one else was following my mark, I snatched the spark plugs out and positioned myself so that I could wait and watch the door without looking suspicious.

After waiting for roughly fifteen minutes, the side door creaked open and I scurried into position with my ass out and head buried under the hood. I fumbled around making lots of noise and then allowed my wrench to drop loudly on the ground.

"Damnit!" I swore sucking on my finger as if I'd hurt it and stamping my foot dramatically.

Styler stopped midway to his car to see what all the commotion was about. When I saw that I had his attention, I shifted my act into high gear. I shook my hand and bent down seductively slow to pick up the wrench with my back toward him, taking care to straighten my legs and show lots of skin on the way up. With a toss of my wig, I turned back to the car with an exasperated look on my face. No sooner had I leaned back under the hood, I could hear Styler's footsteps padding toward me. I couldn't help but smile, as he approached to play his role as "Captain Save a Hoe".

"Hey, baby, you know whatchu' doing under there?" he asked, with a cockiness that made me want to smack the taste out of his mouth.

"My car just stalled out," I whined innocently, "do you think you could take a look at it for me? I don't wanna be late for work."

He looked me over with unshielded lust in his eyes and I played it for everything it was worth. Coyly, I touched his hand. "Sure, baby," he said laughing, "today must be your lucky day."

I laughed good-naturedly as he buried his head under the hood of my Malibu in an attempt to find my non-existent problem. I took another look around to make sure no one was watching us and the coast was still clear. A few minutes later, he stood up and smiled at me.

"It looks like you just need a jump."

"Thank, God," I exclaimed, "I can't afford to put this thing in the shop."

"Well, sweet thing, like I said today is your lucky day. Maybe after I give the car a jump, I'll let you thank me in a special way," he said, openly undressing me with his eyes.

I managed to keep myself from cracking his skull with the wrench I was holding, as I replied deliberately, "Don't make promises you don't intend to keep, Mr…"

"Just call me Ross, baby. Do you have any jumper cables?"

"I think so. Check in the trunk," I said, throwing him the keys.

Watching intensely as he made his way to the trunk, I waited until he stuck his head in to dig around for the cables he would never find. After searching in vain for about thirty seconds, he lifted his head from the opening to ask me a question. I can only assume that he was going to inquire as to where the jumper cables might be, but before he could part his lips to speak I landed a swift flat hand chop to his Adam's apple. His hands instantly flew to his neck. I quickly grabbed him by the back of his head and introduced the bridge of his nose to my knee, knocking him out instantly.

He fell down hard at my feet and I just stood there for a moment staring blankly. Here I was with the man that had raped, tortured, and killed my sister at my feet. The anticipation of how good it was going to feel to finally have my revenge welled up in my stomach. It took a great deal of self-control for me to harness my blood lust enough not to beat him anymore because I didn't have a lot of time to get him into the trunk.

So I set about the task of first lifting his upper torso and then hefting the lower part of his body. Then I applied the handcuffs that I had ready and waiting to his hands and feet. When that task was completed, I stuffed a rag into his mouth followed by a large piece of duct tape. Once I was satisfied with the restraints, I took one last look around and closed the trunk.

"I can't believe it," I said to myself, as I slid behind the driver's seat, "I really did it." At that point the weight of what I was about to do really sunk in. Even though I knew there was still time for me to get out of the car and walk away, I didn't. Rather, I turned the key in the ignition and took off down the street towards my safe haven. The place where he and I could be alone, and once we made it there...for me there would be no turning back.

Chapter 12

"Wake up!" I sang happily smacking Styler in the face. "It's time to start our game!"

His eyes opened with a jolt as he struggled to focus. He tried to sit up but his hands and feet were handcuffed to the metal posts that made up the bed frame. His eyes darted back and forth across the room finally resting on my face. His face showed no signs of recognition as we stared at one another.

After I'd allowed him enough time to take in his surroundings, I swiftly snatched the tape from his mouth. He screamed out in pain and then fixed his black eyes coldly on me.

"Wow!" I retorted sarcastically, "don't you recognize me?"

"No. But what I do know for sure is that you're a dead bitch. I know that for a fact," he said calmly, as his dark eyes bore into mine.

With all the fury I felt burning inside, I cocked back and punched him dead in his mouth knocking out his two front teeth.

"Ahhh!" he cried spitting out teeth and blood.

"I'm very disappointed that you don't recognize me," I said, ignoring the bleeding cut on my knuckles, "but then again the last time you saw me I did look a little different." I walked over to the sink and poured some bottled water over my bloody hand and shook it off, then proceeded to remove the green contacts from my eyes.

"How about now?" I pressed my face close to his so that we were nose to nose. "Do you recognize me now?"

I eased back slowly and watched his eyes light up as the realization of who I was crept into his face. "You're that girl from the courtroom…"

"Yes!" I said excitedly, "Now can you guess why you're here?"

"Look," he began, "I don't know what this is about but…"

"No, no, no…" I said putting my finger to his lips, "There's no need to wonder, because I am going to tell you why. Now be sure to listen carefully because I am only going to go through this once…"

Now that I was sure I had his undivided attention, I began to play with a scalpel I'd purchased for some of the activities I had planned. "Do you remember a girl named Carmen Langston? Sure you do! Well, just in case you didn't know she was my little sister," I stated, while holding the scalpel up to allow the generated light to gleam off of it.

"But I digress…I'm supposed to be telling you why you're here, we'll get to the other stuff later. You are here, Mr. Stlyer, because unfortunately for you, you had the misfortune of killing the wrong girl. If only the justice system would have done what they should have done and put you behind bars for the rest of your life where you belong, we wouldn't be here now. You would be in prison, getting gang raped by Pookie n'em. But that didn't happen and now here we are."

"Look here, bitch..." he began but instantly I was on him like a cat with a swift head butt to the nose and the scalpel positioned inches from his eyes.

"If you interrupt me one more time, I will put this scalpel through your eye! Make no mistake about it, Mr. Styler, this is not a game. Pissing me off will only force me to become more creative in the things I do to torture you."

He flinched visibly at the word "torture" and immediately snapped his mouth shut. "Now...as I was saying," while I continued pointing the scalpel at his eye, "You killed my sister and now you're going to experience everything she experienced up until you decided to take a bat and bash her head in. I have five days of hell planned for you, and it all begins today. Take a look around...," I instructed, as I motioned for him to survey the room.

In the dense generated light, there was a table with various medical utensils, a catheter, bat, and a bedpan. His eyes watered from the blow to the face, as he scanned the room. I felt his body tense beneath me as if the grim realization of his fate finally began to sink in. The handcuffs clinked as he tried to move his hands again.

"Please," he pleaded with a lisp, due to his missing teeth, "I'll give you whatever you want. You obviously know how much money I have. Whatever you want, just please let me go and I'll make it right. Pleassse...don't do thiss."

Looking at him in that pitiful state, with his nose swelling up, two front teeth missing, and handcuffed to a bed became comical to me. I burst out laughing in spite of myself. Ross Styler, a man who had everything and thought he was untouchable was asking for mercy. The irony of the situation was more than I could stand.

"I'm sorry," I choked trying to regain my composure, "I don't mean to laugh at you but really...you gotta admit this is funny. Do you really think that after what you did, you can buy your way out of punishment? Do you know how long I've waited for this day to come?" I screamed, "If I wasn't so determined to make you suffer I would end your miserable life right now and save myself the trouble. But, I've gone through too much trouble to deny myself the pleasure of hearing you beg for mercy. See just then, you asked, but by the time I'm done with you believe me, you will beg.

After regaining my composure, I lifted myself off the bed. His eyes followed me closely as I gingerly placed the scalpel neatly back in its place. Grabbing a dirty rag I had used to clean dirt and cobwebs from my work area and a roll of duct tape, I walked back over to the bed and stood over Styler. He tried to look undaunted but his eyes read of pure terror in anticipation of what I might do next.

"I have to say goodbye for now," I said, as I stuffed the dirty rag in his mouth and secured it again with the duct tape and super glue. "But I'll be back before you know it. I'd try to get some rest if I were you because this is probably the last peaceful night of rest you'll ever have." And with that, I shut off the lights and locked the door behind me, leaving him alone with his thoughts.

Chapter 13

It may sound crazy, but that night I slept like a baby. There were no dreams, no nothing…just peaceful rest. I woke up the next morning to the blaring sound of my telephone ringing, and I knew before I even looked at the caller ID that it was my mother.

"Hello."

"Good morning, Dawn. Were you still asleep?"

"Yes, mother, I'm on vacation."

"Do you know what time it is? Come on it's time to get up. I need you to come over here and help me clean out your sister's room."

At that point I was wide awake, I sat up in my bed and clenched the phone to my ear. "Are you sure, mom? I mean, why today?"

"Why not today?" she asked rhetorically, "Dawn, I've spent many days staring at that closed bedroom door dreading the day I would have to go in there and acknowledge that my baby is really gone. But…I figure it's time to move on and let her go…" she trailed off.

"Mom, you still there?"

"I'm sorry, baby," she said her voice cracking, "I just miss her so much. But, I want to do this and get it over with because no matter how long I wait, it's never going to get any easier."

"Ok, mommy, I'll be there," I promised.

I hung up the phone and silently cursed Ross Styler again for tearing my family apart. Deep down, I really wished that I could've told my mother what I was going to do. I wondered what she would say. Would she condone it or would she turn me in? I only hoped that once the news hit that he was dead, she would finally have closure.

When I finally made it over to my parent's house, my mom was already in Carmen's room knee deep in clothes and other memorabilia. When I walked in, there were photo albums, stuffed animals, and a million other kinds of knick-knacks that Carmen loved to collect laying about.

Tears immediately sprang to my eyes, because I hadn't set foot in that room since the day she died and all at once, a thousand memories of our happiest times flooded my memory. My eyes locked in on a photo that we had taken together on our last trip to Cedar Point, and I bent down to pick it up. She looked so happy in that picture that I couldn't help but smile through my tears.

My mom walked over and hugged me tightly. "Thank you for coming," she said. Overwhelmed by the tremendous lump in my throat, I could only nod as I tried to busy myself with folding clothes and putting them in boxes.

For what seemed like hours, my mother and I worked side by side sorting through Carmen's things. We laughed and cried as we shared memories over various articles that we packed away. With every tear my mother shed, I hated Ross Styler more and more. I couldn't wait to get back to my hideaway so I could start inflicting all the pain I felt on him.

Finally after about five 'o clock, the task was completed. Everything was packed away, except for the photographs that we both agreed should be kept out for everyone. I was so emotionally drained by the time I said good-bye to my mother, it was a relief to finally be free to go back to my apartment to prepare for my evening with Styler.

As I drove home my cell phone rang. The caller ID showed a number I didn't recognize so I sent the call to voicemail. When I arrived at home, I sat down at the table deep in thought. Just as I was about to get up to leave again, my phone beeped signaling a voicemail message. After punching my code to check it, I heard the last voice that I ever expected to hear on the other end; Detective Jones.

"Hello, Ms. Langston, this is Detective Jones. Please give me a call when you get this message."

My palms began to sweat as I hung up the phone. I couldn't imagine why he would be calling me. Did he know what I had done? He couldn't know. I had been so careful. No one saw me kidnap Styler. Or did they? What if I called him back and he demanded I come in for questioning? But, what if I didn't call him back? What would he do then? My mind was racing as I tried to decide what to do.

I couldn't allow myself to go into panic mode, so I sat down and took a deep breath. This was not going to work if I started tripping out every time somebody looked at me crossed-eyed. I had to play it cool. I would call him back and see what he wanted.

"He was probably just calling to check up on me," I told myself, "I'll just wait until tomorrow to call him." With that settled, I walked out the door to begin the first night of my sister's retribution.

Chapter 14

When I arrived at the hideaway, Styler was sleeping. Just standing there watching him rest so peacefully infuriated me, so I dropped the jagged tree branch I was carrying, opened a bottle of water, and poured it in his face.

"Wake up, you bastard," I ordered. His eyes shot open and peered at me with pure hatred. "How did you sleep last night? Oh, I'm sorry I can't hear you...let me take that tape off your mouth," and with that, I snatched the super-glued tape off his mouth taking a sizable swatch of skin with it.

"Owww, you bitch!" he screamed, spit spraying from his mouth, "I swear you're gonna die for this!"

"Rest assured it won't be before you do. Look, I brought you a little present." I held up the sturdy branch I had broken off from a nearby tree, which was about two inches wide and two feet long.

"I know, I know...it's just a regular old branch from a regular old tree, right?" I continued inching closer, "This is a special stick, but before we get into what's going to happen, I wanted to ask you some questions. It's very important for you to answer all of them honestly because if you don't, the stick game is going to get very unpleasant for you."

"I ain't telling you shit," he spat.

Before he could blink, I grabbed the stick like a baseball bat and swung it with all my might, hitting him square in the balls. "I'm so glad to hear you say that," I laughed, while he writhed in pain. Instinctively, he tried to curl up into a ball but the handcuffs on his hands and feet prevented him from doing so. All he could do was rock his body from side to side as tears coursed down his cheeks.

"You miserable bitch…," he cried.

"Oh, baby, it's only just begun. Do you remember how many women you've raped, Styler?" I screamed, "Do you? How many women have you taken advantage of or killed just because you thought you could get away with it?" I punctuated my question with another blow.

No words came, only groans of agony. By this time he was babbling and drooling like a baby. I pulled up my chair and sat down, then waited patiently for the crying and moaning to die down before I proceeded. It took a good ten minutes for him to catch his breath, so that he could stop fidgeting long enough to take his thoughts off his throbbing balls and remember that I was in the room.

"How many women have you raped, Stlyer?"

"I don't…I don't know," he replied between gasps, "I don't remember."

"You don't remember?" I said laughing sarcastically, "How many people have you killed?"

There was a long pause as he tried to freeze out the pain long enough to get his bearings, then he replied weakly, "Ten."

"How many were women?"

"Three."

All I could do was shake my head in disbelief. This man had killed ten people and a jury of his peers put him back on the streets. It made my mind spin to think of all the people taking up jail cells for minor infractions, while murdering rapist drug-dealers like Ross Styler were allowed to remain free. My temper mounted more and more with every passing moment.

"What about my sister?"

"Ohhhh," he moaned writhing back and forth in pain.

"What about my sister?" I spat, "and you better not make me ask you again."

"Your sister," he began, his breathing beginning to return to normal, "I didn't know your sister. I just met her that night at the club…"

"And you decided then that you wanted to rape her, right?" I asked, my anger growing hotter by the second.

"I…"

"Yeah, you raped her first didn't you? You took her to that stanking hole in the ground and you raped her before you did anything else didn't you?"

"Yes," he admitted crying openly.

"Yes…yes you did," I said, dropping the stick and picking up the scissors.

"What are you doing?" he asked frantically.

I said nothing, as I walked over to the bed and began cutting his Versace linen pants from his body. He shook visibly as he tried to adjust himself to see what I was doing. Paying him no mind, I continued to cut through the garment as if I didn't have a care in the world. Once I was done, I removed the silk boxers that hung from his perfectly shaped hips.

As he lay there naked from the waist down, save for his socks, I marveled at how perfectly chiseled his body was. The man was hung like a horse, with a body of a Greek Adonis, he could've had any woman he wanted. What a waste, I thought to myself.

"Do you know what it feels like to be violated, Styler?" I asked, holding the jagged stick up so he could see it. "Do have any idea what it's like to have piping hard flesh plunged into your body over and over again, tearing your insides to shreds? That's what you did to Carmen! If she would've lived through the hell you put her through, she never would have been able to have children! You did that to her!"

"Please...," he pleaded, "I'm sorry..."

"You're not sorry yet, but you will be. You have no idea." I took the stick and positioned it so that it was aimed at my target.

"No!" he screamed.

"Brace yourself," I warned, "you're gonna have to take this one big boy style...no Vaseline."

Without further ado, I plunged that stick into his hind orifice with such force I thought he would break the bed in half from the way he bucked. His shrieks of terror echoed through the basement like sonic waves through hollow caverns. Even after he passed out, I continued to work him over until the tree branch broke off in my hand. I then threw the broken portion to the side and pulled the bloody remaining stump from his body. Holding it over his face, I slapped him until he opened his eyes, so he could see his tattered flesh.

"Did you like that?" I shrieked, "Was it good for you like it was for me?" My voice was so high that I barely recognized it. My adrenaline was pumping so much that I could feel my heart pounding in my ears. Then all of a sudden, I felt sick to my stomach.

Dropping the bloodied stick, I ran outside and vomited. "What am I doing?" I asked myself. I looked back at the open basement door and shook my head. Suddenly, I wanted all of this to be a dream. Just some bad dream that I would wake up from when the alarm clock went off, and Carmen would be asleep in her bed and life would go back to normal.

With my head buried in my hands, I willed my stomach to stop churning and my heart to stop pounding. Before I could stop them, the tears came. Sitting in the grass, crying like a little girl, I thought about Carmen and remembered why I was here.

"I can't fall apart now," I told myself, "he has to pay no matter what. I owe that to her."

It took some time, but I finally regained my composure. With my focus back in tact, I picked myself up and went back into the basement to complete the first night of retribution in memory of my sister.

Chapter 15

When I finally reached the basement, after having my little breakdown, Styler had passed out from what I could only assume was shock. From the look of the stick I had pulled from his badly torn rectum, it looked as though I had done some pretty serious damage. Still, I felt no sympathy for him, so I left him lying there on the mattress in a pool of his own blood.

After I left Styler that night, my whole frame of mind was totally messed up. I still hated him with every fiber of my being, but I also had a nagging feeling of guilt that I was constantly trying to bury beneath my hatred. I had determined a long time ago that nothing, not even my inbred sense of right and wrong, was going to stop me from avenging Carmen's death. I had come way too far to turn back now.

Sleep didn't come easy after I had showered and gotten into bed. So I got back up and sat on my couch to stare out the window, allowing myself to get lost in my thoughts. I thought about everything I still had left to do to Styler before it was finally time to put him out of his misery. It was compelling for me to ask myself whether or not I would have the courage to go through with it when the time came. And honestly at that point, I wasn't sure if the answer would be yes. I hated him, yes...but now that I had him at my mercy, could I take his life in cold blood?

I was so conflicted that I decided it was best not to think about it anymore. That bridge would just have to be crossed when I came to it. Then I turned my thoughts to Detective Jones and why he was calling me. It was with that thought on my brain that I finally fell asleep and woke up with the next morning.

Unnerved by the anxiety festering in the pit of my stomach, I decided against calling the detective back. I concluded that if he really needed to speak with me then he would call back. My conclusion proved accurate because the next morning, in the middle of my daily calisthenics my phone rang and it was him.

After a brief hesitation I answered the phone. "Hello."

"Ms. Langston," he said, "Detective Jones. How are you this morning? I hope I'm not disturbing you by calling so early in the day."

"No," I replied evenly, "What can I do for you, Detective Jones?"

"Well, I was actually hoping to get your answering machine because that would make this a whole lot easier...," he began.

"Yes..." I pressed trying not to sound nervous.

"I wanted to invite you to dinner...with me. I called yesterday, but then you didn't call me back, so I wanted to leave you a more detailed message so that you wouldn't think I was calling about police business," he explained, "I was really hoping to get the answering machine so that if you were going to say no, you could just say it by not calling me back and then I wouldn't feel stupid."

I smiled to myself as I breathed a sigh of relief. He wasn't on to me, he was hitting on me. As funny as the whole situation was to me, at that moment I was flattered, because after all, Detective Jones was fine.

"I would love to have dinner with you, Detective Jones."

"Ok...ok, that's great. Would it be ok for me to pick you up around eight?"

"Let's make it an early dinner and you pick me up at six? I have some things to attend to later this evening."

"Six o'clock it is," he agreed. After taking down my address and directions to my house we ended our call. I sat down and giggled to myself because I was going on a date with the cop that had been trailing the man that killed my sister, who I had kidnapped and planned to kill. The irony was almost more than I could stand.

I must have been crazy to agree to go on that date, but I couldn't deny that I had been attracted to him since day one. Only the circumstances surrounding our meeting were not conducive for dating, and to be honest they still weren't. But after what I had put myself through the night before and not to mention for the past few years, I figured a little bit of me time was just what I needed. And if I could stay close to Jones and keep tabs on what he knew about Styler when news that he was missing came up, then it would be a win-win situation for me.

Like a perfect gentleman, Detective Jones rang my buzzer promptly at six o'clock. Not wanting to appear eager, I called down to let him know that I would be down in a minute as opposed to inviting him into my apartment. After checking my appearance one last time, I went downstairs to add another component to what was probably the most dangerous game I would ever play in my life.

"Well, hello," he greeted, as I stepped out of my building. Before I could reach the bottom of the stairs, he offered his hand to assist me the rest of the way. Once I was on level ground he took my hand, brought it to his lips, and planted a single kiss, his eyes shining with approval. "You look absolutely stunning."

"Thank you," I said silently, appraising him and his attire. He was dressed casually in a pair of black slacks and a neatly tucked button-down shirt. His hair was freshly cut and a small diamond earring gleamed from his left ear. I had to admit he had it going on.

"Thank you for agreeing to go out with me on such short notice."

"Thank you for asking."

"Shall we?" he asked, stepping over to his perfectly detailed black Expedition to open the passenger side door.

On the twenty-minute ride to the restaurant, we had idle conversation about basic things like where we were from and the schools we attended. By the time we reached the restaurant, I had learned that he was born and raised in Detroit, was the middle of three children, and wanted to be a cop like his dad ever since he could walk. The more he told me about himself the more I found myself liking the man, who I could already tell was going to be a huge problem in the grand scheme of things.

We dined at Loving Spoonful, which was one of the premier restaurants in the Detroit area. The atmosphere was elegant and the food was delicious. Our conversation flowed effortlessly as he was a very attentive listener and I found myself very much at ease.

"May I ask you something, Detective Jones?"

"Please, call me Chris, and yes, you can ask me whatever you want."

"Do you date a lot of black girls?"

He sat back in his chair with a slight grin on his face. "That depends on what you consider a lot."

"You know what I mean. Do you date black girls sometimes, almost never, or exclusively?"

"I date whoever I'm interested in at the time, Ms. Langston…"

"Dawn."

"Dawn. I date women I find myself attracted to at the time, and the majority of the time I find that I am attracted to black women most often, but I have dated women of different races, including my own," he replied smiling. "Why do you ask?"

"Just curious. I've never dated a white man before, so I just wanted to know if this was a first for both of us."

"Oh, ok. I can respect that," he responded with obvious amusement. He was so sexy to me at that moment that I found myself wondering what it would be like to kiss him. "So tell me, Dawn, what do you like to do for fun?"

"I like to spar and train," I said, "I'm really in to martial arts."

"Really?"

"Yes. I have always loved the thrill of a good fight. I don't know what it is, but I really love it and I'm good at it. Is that weird?"

"I wouldn't say it's weird. There are a lot of women on the force like that. I think that's why a lot of them became police officers so they could exert some of that energy and get paid for it," he said good-naturedly. "How long have you been in martial arts?"

"For a little over fourteen years. Right now I'm a fourth degree black belt. I've pretty much gone as far as I can go with karate, but I practice some other forms of martial arts that are more prevalent overseas. It keeps me pretty busy."

"What else do you like to do, that's a little more relaxing?"

I thought for a minute and couldn't come up with anything. "I don' know."

"Maybe one day I can show you some of the things I like to do to relax," he offered.

"Like what?" I wanted to know.

"Fishing."

"Fishing?"

"Yeah, my grandfather used to take us fishing all the time and I love it. I go every chance I get," he stated emphatically.

"Where do you go to fish when you live in Detroit?" I asked, genuinely interested.

"Ahhh, that's for me to know and you to find out. If I tell you all my secrets now, how will I get you to go out with me again?"

"Good point," I said laughing. It was the best time I'd had in a while and all too soon we found ourselves back in the car on the way back to my apartment.

"Thank you for a lovely evening," I said, after we'd pulled up to the front of my building. "I had a really nice time."

"Me too," he responded, "would it be ok for me to call you again sometime?"

"I'd like that. Goodnight, Chris," I said, closing the door behind me. I didn't look back as I walked into my building because I knew he was watching me. When I got upstairs I looked out the window and saw that he was still sitting there. So I flicked the light to let him know that I'd made it in ok. As I watched him pull off, I wondered how I was going to keep this man from getting too close to me, because in spite of myself I was looking forward to seeing him again already.

Chapter 16

After having such a wonderful night with Detective Jones, it took a while for me to get back into the proper frame of mind to visit Styler. Being that it was already Wednesday, I only had a few days left to do what I had to do, so I couldn't afford to waste time. It would only be a matter of time before his brother took notice of his absence, if he hadn't already, and put an all points bulletin out on the streets.

The evenings that we would spend together from this point on would be very intense and mentally challenging for me, so I didn't rush myself in getting prepared. I fell deep into meditation that would allow me to focus on my mission. If I was going to be successful, there could be no more moments of weakness like the one I experienced the night before. The journey ahead was only going to get harder, and I owed it to my sister to be strong.

Once I had reaffirmed my objective, I packed a bag and drove over to the hideaway. When I opened the basement door, the smell of urine hit me in the face like a hammer. I said nothing, as I set about starting up the generator so I could turn the lights on. Styler's eyes were open and followed me around the room emanating a glare of pure hatred. He couldn't talk because I had replaced the tape on his mouth, sans the super glue, but I'm sure if he could, he would have had some very choice words.

"You don't look happy to see me!" I teased, meeting his heated gaze. "Did you piss on yourself,

Styler? How's your ass?" Laughing to myself, I continued to prepare for the evening's festivities. When I was finished, I grabbed a bottled water and pulled a chair up to the bed.

I allowed his anticipation to mount before I made any movement, then I gingerly opened the bottled water and brought it to my lips as if to drink it. As he zeroed in on the bottle, the look in his eyes changed instantly from hatred to lust. It had been two days since he had anything to drink. When I was sure I had his undivided attention, I took a long exaggerated swig.

"Ummm, this water is so refreshing," I said, smacking my lips loudly.

Frustrated, he turned his head to the wall. Undaunted, I continued to drink loudly and enjoy my water until the whole sixteen-ounce bottle was empty.

"Ok, now that I've wet my whistle, we can begin," I announced, to the back of his head. "Styler, do you hear me talking to you? I would hate to think that you're ignoring me." I only had to wait for about fifteen seconds before he finally turned back to face me.

"I'm so glad you turned back on your own. You really wouldn't have wanted me to call your name again. Anyway, we are going to have a discussion before we move on with our daily activities," I stated. "I'm sure that you know by now that any lack of participation on your part, will result in me tearing in to you earlier than the appointed time. Do you understand?" Without hesitation, he nodded his head in agreement.

"Good. Now, together you and I are going to make a list of all the people you have killed. After the list has been completed, you and I are going to write a letter to all of the families of those people admitting to what you did. You are going to do this before you die so that those families can have closure. Is that clear?" I asked and again he nodded in agreement. "Great. Now for the tape..."

Swiftly before he could blink, I snatched the tape from his mouth again, and as before, he cried out in agony. Though I didn't super glue the tape to his face, the tape itself was still strong enough to reawaken the initial wound.

"Sorry," I retorted, sitting back to grab my notebook and pen. "Now, due to time constraints we are only going to do the list today. We'll work on the letters tomorrow. Now let's start with victim number one."

There was a long silence while he stared off into space. Just when I was about to remind him about my non-compliance rule, he began to speak. "The first person I ever killed was Thomas Green."

"Why?"

"It was part of my initiation into a gang. I was seventeen," he said in a hushed voice, "We had to pick a random person and stop them in their car to ask for directions. And when they stopped to give directions we had to shoot them. I only know his name because I looked for the story in the newspaper."

"And number two?" I asked, through clenched jaws.

"Jonathan Wimberly. He was a drug deal gone bad."

"Three?"

"Travis Stevenson," he chuckled deliriously, "he tried to cheat my brother out of some money, so I had to smoke his ass."

"Go on."

"Eric Stokes, Willie Johnson, and Jay Spencer. Those were all dealers that worked for us. They slipped up, so they got hit. I take care of that stuff from time to time because my brother don't really like to get his hands dirty. I never minded though," he admitted.

"What about the three women?" I pressed. He simply stared at the ceiling and said nothing. My anger toward him only increased my impatience, and before I could stop myself I had jumped up and slapped him across the face. "Answer me!" I shouted.

"The first woman I ever killed...her name was Tracy Martinez."

"Why?"

"I killed her because I thought she was cheating on me."

"And the second woman?"

"Her name was... I don't even know her name. She got smoked when we hit Willie and Jay. She was just in the wrong place at the wrong time."

"And the last one?"

"You know who that last one was," he said, nervously taking care to keep his eyes averted from mine.

"I want to hear you say it."

"Her name was Carmen."

"Say her whole name," I ordered.

"Carmen Langston."

"And why did you kill her?" I asked, tears welling up in my eyes.

Styler pursed his lips together and said nothing as he continued to stare at the ceiling. Then after what seemed like an eternity, he turned and looked me in the eye and said, "I didn't have a reason for killing your sister. I saw her and I wanted her. When I tried to talk to her and she brushed me off, I still wanted her and then I wondered what it would be like to kill her just because I could...so I did."

My body trembled as tears of rage and disgust ran down my cheeks and splattered on the floor. To hear the words that had just spewed forth from his mouth was more than I could bear. Any guilt that I may have felt about what I was doing evaporated that very instant, and I knew right then that I would gladly spend the rest of my life in prison just to have the satisfaction of murdering this man. To see the expressionless look on his face, as he talked about the people he killed, was enough to make me want to put a bullet through his head and save myself the trouble. I actually thought that maybe he was trying to provoke me to do just that, so he wouldn't have to experience all of the other horrible things I had waiting for him in the days to come.

"Well, Ross, your day of redemption has arrived," I said, wiping the tears from my eyes, "so let's get started shall we?"

After pulling myself together, I picked up the scalpel and held it up for him to see. "Do you remember the plug of skin you bit out of Carmen's thigh? Well," I continued without waiting for a response, "I don't intend to let my lips touch your disgusting flesh so I'll be using this."

Setting the scalpel aside, I picked up a miniature blowtorch and held it up to his face. "Since you don't have enough hair for me to pull out, I figured I would burn a couple of patches into your scalp for you," I explained. Then I pulled out a pair of razor sharp wire cutters and laid them on his belly. "These are for the finale before the grand finale. I'm almost sure you know what that's going to be. Don't you?"

For the briefest second I saw a flicker of fear in his eyes, but then he looked at me with his mangled face and smiled a toothless grin. "You think what you're doing to me is going to bring your sister back? It ain't. Yeah, I killed all those people, and didn't think twice about it. What about you? You think you can do all this to me and go on with your life? People like you don't have the make up for what it takes to be a killer. That's what makes us different," he said calmly, "I'm a predator, and people like you and your sister are prey. So you go ahead and do what you need to do to make yourself feel better, but you really have to ask yourself at the end of the day…will you be able to live with it?"

The magnitude of what he said registered deep within my soul. I thought about the minor lapses I had experienced earlier that day and the day before, and I wondered what impact it would have on me after it was all said and done. But only briefly. The moment passed almost as soon as it began and before I knew it, I had grabbed the scalpel and plunged it deep into the meaty flesh of his right thigh.

"I'm sure I'll learn to live with it," I said over his agonizing shrieks, "you'd be surprised at how quickly I can adapt."

Chapter 17

Styler's screams of agony echoed in my brain and the stench of burning flesh lingered in my nostrils, as I lay in bed that night. It was almost four a.m. and sleep eluded me like a thief in the night. Opting for a cup of hot tea to soothe my nerves, I padded into the kitchen to start the teakettle.

As I reached into the cabinet to grab the tea bags, I glanced over the counter and noticed that my answering machine was blinking to indicate messages. There were four; one from Christopher saying what a good time he had and the other three were from my mother.

"Dawn, I was just calling to see how you were doing. Call me," was the first message.

"Dawn, this is mom again. I have a nagging feeling that I just can't seem to get rid of and I don't know why. So, honey, please call me when you get in, just so I know you're alright," was the second.

The third message was borderline frantic with her ordering that I quit being inconsiderate and call her right away, before she called the police to report me as a missing person. So, I figured in the interest of keeping the police from prying into my affairs anymore than necessary, I'd better call her back before she had a heart attack.

"Hello," my mother's strained voice drifted through the phone after the first ring.

"Hi, mom," I said, "I know it's late, but I just got your messages and didn't want you to worry."

"Dawn, where the hell have you been?" she barked. "I have been calling you all evening; your cell phone and your home phone. What is going on over there? Your father and I have been worried sick about you!"

"Mom, calm down, I went to dinner with a friend and when I came home I was tired so I went straight to bed. I turned my ringers off so I wouldn't be disturbed, that's all. I'm sorry if I scared you."

"Thank goodness! I didn't know what to think!" she sighed with relief. With that catastrophe out of the way, she immediately turned her attention to my dinner date. "And who did you go to dinner with?"

"Just a friend, mommy. Look, I'll tell you all about it in the morning. It's late and you need to get some rest. I just wanted to call you and let you know that everything was ok, alright?"

"Ok, baby," she relented, "I love you and I'll talk to you tomorrow." Thankfully she hung up after that and I was free to sit and enjoy my tea in peace. I relished the thought because I knew that when she finally got me on the phone, she was going to brow beat me until I told her all about my date.

That in and of itself was a whole other issue. I wasn't sure how my parents would react to the fact that I had gone out with a police officer. Not to mention that he was a police officer that worked on my sister's case and he was white.

"Should be interesting," I said to myself.

Even though I didn't remember falling asleep, I woke up the next morning feeling refreshed. It was almost ten thirty, so I figured I would call my mother and get the third degree out the way so the rest of my day could be worry free.

"Hello," my dad greeted on the other end of the receiver.

"Hi, daddy. How are you this morning?" I asked, smiling in spite of myself. I had always loved to hear my daddy's voice. It was so proud and strong, like he was ten feet tall. When I was a little girl, I always felt like nothing could harm me when my daddy was around. In my eyes, my father was the epitome of everything that a man was supposed to be.

"I'm ok, baby girl. How you doing, besides almost giving your mother a heart attack yesterday?" he inquired, with a note of seriousness that was not lost on me.

"I'm fine, daddy. I just fell asleep that's all."

"I know you don't mean nothing by it, Dawn, but you need to be a little more thoughtful towards your mother. I know you feel like you're just living your life, but she's been through a lot…you both have. I hope you never have to find out what it feels like to lose a child. I'm not coming down on you, just asking you to be a little more considerate. Call and check in once in a while to let us know you're doing ok. Ok?"

Immediately, I was ashamed of myself. I had been so caught up in my own twisted obsession with revenge I had been all but neglecting my parents. I had to bite down on my trembling lip to keep from crying. I hated it when my dad was upset with me. "I'm sorry, daddy," I said, "I'll do better, I promise."

"I know you will, baby girl," he replied, in a lighter tone to assure me that all was forgiven, "hold on and I'll get your mother for you."

"Well good morning, baby, I didn't expect to hear from you this early," my mother chimed merrily, after she picked up the phone.

"I wanted to catch you early to see if I could take you to lunch."

"I think I might like that, Dawn! It's been awhile since you and I have gone out and spent quality time together," she said happily, "what time should I be ready?"

"I'll be there to pick you up around twelve-thirty. Is that ok?"

"That's fine, I'll be ready. See you in a little bit."

I hung up the phone and smiled to myself. Even though I knew my mother was going to spend the whole afternoon drilling me about my dinner date, I couldn't wait for us to spend some alone time together outside of the house. There were too many memories there. I wanted to see her laugh and smile again like she used to.

As promised, she was ready and waiting when I got to the house. After a quick hello and goodbye to daddy, we piled into the car and headed out. First, I surprised her going to the mall to buy her some new clothes and then we went to a movie. After the show, we had lunch at her favorite Thai food restaurant in Southfield.

For the major part of our day, I had managed to avoid the dinner date conversation I had been dreading.

Then my phone rang while we were seated at the lunch table. I checked my caller ID and it was Chris. I didn't want to keep putting him off, so I answered and spoke long enough just to let him know that I was out with my mother and would call him back later.

"Who was that?" my mother inquired, trying to appear nonchalant.

"A friend," I teased.

"A friend, huh. Have I ever met this friend?"

"As a matter of fact you have."

"Really?" she asked, gearing up for the challenge I had so effortlessly set her up for.

"Yes, you've met him a few times, actually."

I could almost see the wheels turning in her head as she tried to wrack her brain to figure out who my mystery man could possibly be, but she continued to draw a blank. There had only been a minimal amount of male companionship in my life since my high school and college days, because most of the guys I dated either irritated me with their weakness after awhile or became intimidated by my lust for competitive fighting and training. It didn't really bother me too much because I came to understand one thing about myself when it came to relationships…I tended to have the mentality of a man when it came to romance. Because if and when I had time for a relationship, once I got what I wanted from a guy, I became easily bored.

Finally, after a while she gave up. "I have no idea who it could be," she admitted.

Taking a deep breath, I mentally prepared myself for the maelstrom that was sure to follow. "I had dinner with Detective Jones," I said casually, like it was no big deal.

"Detective Jones...isn't that the one who worked on your sister's case?"

"Yes."

"The white one?"

"That's the one."

"Is it serious?"

"Mom, we just went to dinner. How could it be?"

"Oh," she said, as she toyed with her napkin. She was obviously at a loss for words, which was something that I was totally unprepared for. "Well...was he nice?"

"Yes, mommy, he was very nice. Very well mannered, interesting...not typical. I think I might like to see him again," I admitted. "How do you feel about that?"

"What about you dating a cop, or about you dating a white man?"

"Both."

She looked thoughtfully at me for a moment and then smiled. "I think that if you like him, then we might just have to have him over to the house for dinner. I mean who's safer for you to be dating than a cop, right? I know I'll sleep better at night knowing that you're with someone who can protect you."

I had to touch my face to make sure that my mouth wasn't open. I was speechless. This certainly was not the reaction I expected, but I welcomed it just the same.   The rest of our afternoon went very pleasantly after that.

      After dropping my mother off, I could barely wait to get home to call Chris, so I could see what the rest of the evening had to offer.

Chapter 18

I had butterflies in my stomach as I held the phone to my ear, waiting for Chris to answer. After the fourth ring, his voicemail picked up telling me he was unavailable and would call back at his first opportunity.

Disappointed, I hung the phone up and sat on the couch. I turned on the television to try to occupy the idle time that would linger until it was time for me to go back to my hideout. As I sat there watching the news with all the horrific stories that plague the media everyday, I felt a knot of anger developing in the pit of my stomach. For the life of me, I could not understand how people could be so vile. And even more disturbing than that is that our justice system is so flawed. It continuously allows criminals to run rampant, while countless undeserving people are behind bars serving ridiculously long sentences simply because their skin is the wrong color.

Before I could get completely lost in my contempt for the American justice system, my phone rang. The caller ID confirmed that it was the call I'd been waiting for, so I picked it up on the third ring.

"Hello."

"Hello, are you still busy?" he asked, that sexy voice caressing my ear through the telephone.

"No, actually I was just sitting here watching the news. How are you?"

"I'm good. Better now that I'm talking to you."

A smile crept to my lips as I sat down to get comfortable. "To what do I owe the pleasure of this phone call, Detective Jones?"

"I was calling to see if you felt like getting beat up in some bowling tonight," he said in a cocky tone.

"I beg your pardon, but do you know who you're talking to? If there is ever any beating to be done, nine times out of ten I'm the one doing it. So if you're challenging me, you better come correct," I shot back matching his cockiness.

"Oh, you ain't said nothing but a word. You and me, Cherryhill Lanes, six 'o clock sharp. Don't be late."

"I won't be late, just don't chicken out," I taunted.

"Loser buys dinner…"

"So make sure you don't forget your wallet," I said, hanging up before he could say anymore.

I arrived at the bowling alley promptly at six. When I entered the building, I spotted Chris immediately, sitting on a barstool at an empty lane.

"Hey," I said tapping him on the shoulder.

"Hey," he grinned, "you ready for your spanking?"

"We'll see," I said, brushing past him to find a ball.

We battled neck and neck for two games straight. He won the first round with a score of 170, and I won the second with a 175. His competitiveness was almost as bad as mine, which was a complete turn on for me. By the time we got to the tenth frame of the third game, we were both laughing so hard and talking so much junk, it was a miracle we were able to keep the ball out of the gutter. Needless to say, I held it together long enough to win. I was glad to see that he was a gracious loser.

"Good game, Detective," I said, holding my hand out.

"You know I let you win right?" he asked, shaking my extended hand good-naturedly.

Chuckling, I shrugged my shoulders and began to unlace my bowling shoes. "So where are you taking me to eat?"

"You're the winner, so we go where ever you want to go."

"Really? Ok then, I want the greasiest hamburger and fry combo your money can buy with a big vanilla milkshake on the side."

"You got it," he laughed.

We ended up in the bowling alley restaurant eating off of styro-foam plates soaked with grease. The hamburger was the best I'd eaten in a while because being the health fanatic that I was, I didn't typically eat that kind of food. My mouth was in heaven, but I knew I'd pay for it later.

"How's your burger?" he inquired, with a smirk on his face.

"This is soooo good," I gushed, savoring every greasy morsel that went down my throat.

For the next hour or so, we sat there joking around and talking about nothing and everything all at the same time. I still couldn't believe how comfortable I felt around him. I had to keep reminding myself that he was still a cop and I had to be careful. If he ever got wind of what I was doing there would still be trouble. At the thought of that, I looked at my watch and saw that it was after ten. I knew I still had work to do, so I excused myself by saying it was getting late and I should be getting home.

"Ok, just let me take care of the bill and then I'll walk you to your car," he said.

As we walked side by side, I glanced at him from the corner of my eye. He was so handsome, and seemed so strong and confident. It felt good to be in the presence of a man who could make me feel safe, even though I was a woman with more than enough resources to defend herself.

As I listened to our footsteps echo in sync on the pavement, I wondered what he would think of me if he knew what I was capable of. What would he think if he knew I had a man handcuffed to a bed in the basement of an abandoned house, that I visited on a nightly basis to torture and emasculate? Involuntary shame crept into my heart at the thought of him ever finding out what I had done.

"This is me," I said stopping next to my Malibu.

"Alright...Ms. Langston. Until next time," he said, smiling down at me, "I'm off tomorrow night, so I was wondering if I could take you out again?"

"As much as I would love to say yes, I already have plans for tomorrow evening..."

"Oh," he said sounding disappointed.

"...but, I'm free on Saturday. In fact, we could plan a whole day for Saturday."

"Ok," he replied, "that's even better. What time should I pick you up?"

"How about twelve."

"Twelve it is. See you then." We stood awkwardly for a long moment and then he gently lifted my chin and kissed me softly on the lips. "Good night, Dawn."

"Goodnight," I replied. I unlocked my car and he opened the driver's side door so I could get in and then closed it securely behind me.

Trying not to appear flustered, I put the car in gear and drove off towards home. Before turning out of the parking lot, I looked into my rearview mirror and saw that he was still standing in the same spot staring after me. I knew that I was being silly, but I couldn't stop myself from wondering what he was thinking about. I didn't dwell on it, but I knew that I was really starting to like him and that meant I would need to have my guard up from that point on. I couldn't allow my heart to write a check that my ass wasn't willing to cash.

Chapter 19

When I finally made it to the hideout, I sat in my car for a long while. I was thinking about the magnitude of the journey that still lay ahead. It was Thursday, and Friday was the day Styler was scheduled to die. My mind, body, and soul were totally in agreement with the thought that the end of his life would more than repay his debt to Carmen and the rest of society, but there was still a small part inside of me that cried out to my conscious. And once again, I reminded myself of my promise to my dead sister to seek revenge on the man that tore our family apart.

In an effort to rekindle the blind hatred I needed to feel toward this man to do what I needed to do, I summoned mental pictures of Carmen's mutilated corpse to remind me how much Ross Styler deserved to suffer. After dozens of mental flashes of what could only be referred to as the worst day of my life, my anger was sufficiently ignited enough for me to go into the basement.

When I turned on the lights, Styler stirred slightly from the brightness. The movement he made caused a deep groan to escape from deep down inside. Once my eyes adjusted to the light, even I had to shudder from his appearance, as I removed the tape from his mouth. His nose was swollen black and blue across the bridge spreading underneath his eyes. In addition to the two missing front teeth that could be plainly seen, he now also had three puckering boils on his head from where I had burned patches of his hair. Aside from the injuries on the upper part of his body, he was still naked from the waist down. His balls were still visibly bruised from where I'd hit him with the stick, and there was a big bloody gaping wound on his right thigh where I'd carved out a patch of skin. And to top it all off, even though he reeked of piss, after all I'd done to him, he still had managed not to defecate on himself, which was amazing to me.

Disgusted by the sight of him, I turned to find the items I would need for the night, and then I settled into my chair beside the bed. His dark eyes focused on me intently, not with hardness or anger but with anticipation of more pain.

"Are you ready to do these letters?" I asked pointedly.

He shook his head solemnly and turned his face to the wall.

"I guess we'll start from the top and go in order of how you named them off yesterday. I want you to speak the words that you want me to write in each letter. You will explain to each victim's family why you killed their loved one and then you will ask for their forgiveness. Is that understood?" Again he nodded his agreement.

"Well," I sighed impatiently, "what are you waiting for. Thomas Green, let's get on with it. To the family of Thomas Green is how it will begin...let's go..."

"To the family of Thomas Green," he began slowly, "I am sorry for the loss I have imposed on your family..." and from there he dictated what seemed to be a very sincere letter of apology to the family of the first person he had ever murdered.

The longer he talked the more grieved he became. A few times he would try to soften what he had done, but I chastised him each time by reminding him what the consequences of his dishonesty would be. By the time we'd made it to the fourth letter, his face was wet with tears, as he recounted all the horrible things he had done while expressing his deepest apologies to the families of his victims.

When we got to letters five through nine, he was virtually incoherent as he continued to babble apologies. It was as if the floodgates had been opened and he didn't know how to close them. He was so pitiful by that time, I almost felt sorry for him. I didn't know if it was the torture he had endured for the past three days, or if by some stroke of irony, deep down inside he really felt guilty about the things he had done.

Then finally, it was time for him to address what he had done to Carmen. It was at this point I made him stop to sign each of the nine letters we had just completed.

Cautiously, I took the keys to the handcuffs out of my pocket and sat on the edge of the bed. Looking him straight in the eye, I held his gaze for a long moment.

"Now, I am going to free one of your hands so that you can sign these letters," I explained, "If I even think that you're going to try something stupid, I will set you on fire. Do you believe me?" I asked and he nodded. "Good.   Now are you right handed or left handed?"

"Right," he replied weakly.

With the key in my hand, I reached over and freed his right hand. His hand shook tremendously as he scribbled his signature on each of the letters I placed before him. When the task had been completed, I re-cuffed his right hand and sat back in my chair. After folding each letter and placing it neatly into a blank envelope, I looked at Styler expectantly.

"Now, I want you to tell me about the night you kidnapped Carmen," I demanded.

He eyed me nervously as if weighing his options. I returned his gaze with a hard glare, my face expressionless. I was determined to keep my face neutral so not to scare him into lying or leaving out key details.

"Don't worry," I assured him, "the longer I listen to you talk, the less you have to worry about me hurting you. So talk. I want to know everything. From the time you met her at the club up until the moment you took her life."

He closed his eyes as if trying to recreate that night in his mind and then he began to speak. "I saw her when she first walked into the club. She was so beautiful. I remember she had a certain innocence about her that excited me. After watching her with her friends for about a half hour, I wanted her so bad that I actually approached her myself, instead of having one of my boys send her to me."

"I started out with some small talk and then I asked her if I could buy her a drink, and she said 'no'. Then I asked her if she wanted to dance and she told me 'no' again. I was pissed, but didn't want to lose it so I said ok and went back to my seat. As the night went on, I still couldn't take my eyes off her. Then at about eleven 'o clock I saw her head toward the door, so I followed her outside."

My jaw tightened as he went on. "I caught up with her she was about to get in to her car. I tried to talk to her again and she just kept brushing me off, telling me she was tired and just wanted to go home. She asked me why I couldn't see that she just wasn't interested and that's when I lost it. Before I knew it, I..."

"You what," I pressed angrily.

"I...I punched her in the face and knocked her out. I looked around the parking lot to make sure that no one had seen me and then I dragged her to my car and put her in the back seat. I began to panic a little because I didn't mean to hit her, I just wanted to talk to her. I didn't know what I was going to do, so I just jumped in my car and started driving. After I had drove around for about forty-five minutes, I came across an abandoned building that crack-heads used to shoot up in, so I thought I would just dump her there and drive off but she started waking up.

"So, I grabbed her out of the car and dragged her into the building. I went all the way down to the basement just in case she started to scream or something. By the time I got her down there, she had woke up and started trying to fight me, so I threw her down on the bed and held her down so she couldn't hit me anymore but she kept struggling. I just remember holding her there and thinking how beautiful she was, and how I wanted to smash that beauty to pieces because she had rejected me. By that time I was so turned on that I couldn't resist..." he said, fading out.

"You couldn't resist what!" I shouted, smacking him across the face.

"You know what," he replied his voice cracking, "don't make me do this! If you're going to kill me just kill me!"

"I'm going to kill you! You don't have to worry about that! But I want you to tell me before you die, with your own filthy lips, about how you violated, tortured, and then murdered my sister!" I screamed. "If you don't, so help me God, I will skin you alive! Now you tell me and you tell it all, and don't make me tell you again!"

"I RAPED her, ok! She wouldn't give it to me, so I took it," he threw back, tears streaming down his cheeks, "and I loved every minute of it. Being inside of her was better than being high. By the time I was done with her, she had passed out again and I went outside to get my handcuffs. I cuffed her to the bed, until I could figure out what I was going to do with her.

"I don't know why I didn't just leave her there, but the more I stared at her beautiful face, the more I wanted to destroy it. If she didn't want me, I was going to make sure that no one ever wanted her again. No woman had ever resisted me like she did. I couldn't take it, and the more I thought about it the madder I got. Then I ran out to my car and drove off so I could calm myself down.

"The next day when I came back, she was awake and her eyes were red and swollen from crying and her throat was hoarse from screaming for help. When she saw me, she spit at me and started calling me all kinds of names, promising that I would never get away with what I did to her. I didn't like being threatened, so I started pulling her hair. Her screams excited me so I tried to kiss her and she bit my lip, and so I bit her back on her chest and her thigh to see how she liked it. That only made her go crazier and she starting bucking and kicking…getting out of control so I punched her again to knock her out. Then I taped her mouth shut so I wouldn't have to listen to her mouth anymore. When I tasted the blood on my lip, I looked down and saw what I had done to her breast and thigh, it gave me a rush…and it scared me so I left. That time I stayed away for a couple of days, so I could try to figure out what to do."

Tears streamed silently down my face as he continued, "During the two days that I was away, I tried to figure out what to do. Tried to figure out what was wrong with me. I have always known that I wasn't normal, but I had never done anything like this before. I felt bad about it, but at the same time it was an adrenaline rush to me. I knew I couldn't let her go because she would go to the police, and I couldn't tell my brother because he would have tripped out on me. He only killed people when it was necessary because he didn't like bringing attention to his organization. So I was on my own. When I finally went back to the spot, I tried to talk to her to see if she would just forget the whole thing happened if I let her go, but she just gave me the finger. That's when I went to my car and got my wire cutters and cut off her two fingers. I just wanted to get the middle finger but it was too hard to get to, so I had to take the first one too..."

By this time, I was so blinded by rage that I was trembling. My jaw ached from grinding my teeth, but I didn't stop him from finishing his story. "She began choking on vomit because her mouth was still taped, and then she passed out again. I left again and went to tend to some other business I had to take care of. But I knew in the back of my mind that I could never let her leave. I knew that I couldn't use my gun to finish her off because that would have easily been traced back to me no matter how I disposed of it. So, when I came back the next day I brought my baseball bat. And I used it to..."

"Stop! Stop it!" I screamed covering my ears. My mind was reeling from what I'd just heard. I relived every moment of Carmen's terror as he recounted everything he'd done to her. I had to walk away to collect myself because I couldn't stop the tears from pouring from my eyes.

I hated that man with every fiber of my being. There were no words to describe the magnitude of my hatred for him. There was no rhyme or reason for any of the murders he had committed, and by far my sister's had been the worse. At that point, I knew without a doubt that I was doing the right thing.

Grabbing the tape, I replaced the gag back over his mouth. Through my tears, I saw my way to the table to get my shiny new razor-sharp wire cutters. "You know, Stlyer," I said wiping my eyes. I grabbed his left hand and turned it palm side down so that his fingers were accessible, "I'm glad we had this talk." From that moment on, there was no more talking.

Chapter 20

I spent the better part of the next morning on the computer researching Styler's other victims and trying to find contact information for them, so that I could mail the letters. From what I could find online, he hadn't lied about the details of the murders. Of course the media had left out some of the more graphic details.

After five hours, I had located addresses for six of the nine people, besides Carmen, that he had killed. Since my eyes were beginning to throb from staring at the LCD screen, I decided to take a break.

As I sat back in my chair, I looked thoughtfully at the little tin box that sat on the table in front of me. After I had severed Styler's middle and index fingers, I put them into the little tin box and packed it with dry ice. It was my intention, to gift wrap the box and its contents and have it delivered to his brother's club. Then he would know that his little brother wasn't so untouchable after all.

After hearing all the dreadful details of what he did to my sister, I no longer had any reservations about ending his life. That man was the scum of the earth and I was sure that hell would welcome him with open arms. My only regret was that I would not be there to personally see the look on his brother's face when he opened my little gift box. The thought of it brought a smile to my face.

Taking special care to address the envelopes with gloves and a typewriter straight from the box, like I had seen in the movies, I systematically dropped each of them into a zip-lock bag after they were finished. I didn't want to chance having any incriminating stray fibers from my body or anything else getting on the envelopes by laying them on the table. Once that was finished, I drove all the way to Birmingham to mail them.

With that out of the way, all that was left to do was to pay Nico Styler a visit. I changed into my disguise and went into a specialty shop to order another elaborate flower bouquet made out of cookies. I had it packaged in such way that I was able to put the neatly wrapped package in the center and arrange the flower cookies festively around it. Then when I got in the vicinity of the club, I found a pimply-faced teenager and paid him twenty bucks to take it in and drop it off. I knew that Nico was used to people kissing his ass, so receiving a gift of that sort would be nothing out of the ordinary for him.

I knew the Nico would not make his appearance at the club until later that night. So after I watched the kid go in with my bouquet and come back out empty handed, I got back into my car and prepared to go home. I wanted to wait until the kid was safely out of dodge before I pulled off, but then to my surprise, Nico Styler pulled up in his Lexus convertible and went into the club.

My curiosity gnawed at me. I watched the door and wondered how the scene would unravel when Nico went into his office and opened the package that was sure to be sitting on his desk by now. Unable to stand the anticipation, I walked into the club and took a seat at the bar. After ordering a rum and coke to sip on, I began to watch the door that I was sure led to Nico's office in the mirror behind the bar. As I sat there, I tried to imagine what he was doing at that very moment.

Sipping slowly to prolong my stay until the fireworks went off, I watched silently but nothing happened. "He must be pre-occupied," I thought, as I finished my drink and slid off the barstool. Fifteen minutes had gone by and nothing. I was tired of waiting so I got back in my car and left. He would find my little present soon enough.

I felt oddly detached from the whole situation as I drove down the road. I knew that in a few hours I was going to murder a man in cold-blood yet it still didn't seem real. I thought about Christopher and wondered if I was going to be able to look him in the eye again. It was of no use for me to think about that right then, I decided I would just have to cross that bridge when I came to it.

Chapter 21

Before I knew it, the appointed time had arrived and I found myself back at the abandoned house, sitting in my car with a baseball bat in my hands. It felt so heavy as I sat there staring into the night.

A battle was raging within me and the ruckus it was causing in my head made me feel sick. Flashes of Styler raping Carmen, biting her flesh, and various other unspeakable horrors played over and over in my mind. Then it switched to flashes of me cutting Styler, ravaging him with the tree branch, cutting off his fingers, and every other thing I had done to punish him. Salty tears of anger and frustration streamed down my cheeks, as I tried to push it all out of my mind.

Angrily, I pushed the car door open and made my way toward the basement entrance. With each step that took me closer to the door, my righteous anger rose vehemently into my soul urging me on. By the time I opened the door, I was mentally ready, willing, and able to do what I had come to do.

Styler's eyes were closed when I turned on the lights. I didn't know if he was unconscious from loss of blood or asleep. I couldn't imagine that he could have been sleeping with all the pain he had to have been in. He looked a mess. His broken nose was still badly swollen and the wounds from where I had cut his flesh away seemed to be seeping. Blood had congealed around the stumps that once held his fingers, as his hand hung limply from the handcuffs.

He had a weird expression on his once handsome face from having to try to breathe through a broken nose. And to top it all off, the arid stench of feces wafted up to my nostrils, acknowledging that he had finally soiled himself, which was something I found to be very comical, given his past display of arrogance.

"Wake up, Ross," I said, calmly poking him with the bat. I waited patiently while he stirred and slowly opened his eyes. "Are you ready to die?"

Jolted to full alertness by my question, he focused nervously on the baseball bat I had just poked him with and shook his head violently from side to side. "What?" I asked sweetly, "Do you have something to say?" Amused by his blatant show of fear, I snatched the tape from his mouth and allowed him to plead his case.

Flinching from the pain in his face he coughed a few times, and after a few moments was finally was able to catch his breath. "Please," he begged, tears of self-pity spilling over onto the bed, "please...I'm sorry. I'm begging you, please don't kill me. I don't want to die..."

I said nothing, as I watched him continue to come unraveled right before my eyes. "I don't know why I did it!" he cried. "I'm sick. I know that now. I'm sick and I deserve everything you did to me. Now I know the kind of pain I put those people through, and I'm sorry. Just please...let me go. I'm begging you...please...forgive me."

I probably could have listened to him ramble on for a good long while had he not said those last two words. It was at that point that I completely lost it.

"How dare you ask me for forgiveness!" I screamed, swinging the bat hitting him squarely on his kneecap, crushing it.   "The person you need to be begging for forgiveness isn't here right now! So you'll have to leave a message at the sound of the beep!" And with that, I hit him again for emphasis, crushing the other kneecap. His howls of pain resonated in my ears, fueling my anger.

My adrenaline was pumping so hard and fast that I felt like my heart was going to explode. "You got a lot of nerve, you know that?" I went on crazily. "Do you have any idea what you've done to our family? My mother and father have basically sentenced themselves to confinement because they've all but lost their will to leave the house anymore! My mother has slipped into a severe state of depression and has to be doped up all the time! My father has turned into a shell of his former self, and let's not even start on me!"

"Do you want to know how I've been dealing with the loss of my sister, Styler?" I shrieked, hitting him in the stomach with the butt of the bat. "I haven't had a life since she's been gone, do you know why? Because I have devoted my every waking moment to training, saving money, preparing, and waiting for the day that I could make you pay for what you did. My sister was my best friend! You took the best part of me when she died. She was all that was beautiful and good inside of me. You see, I'm not good Styler! I love violence. I love to inflict pain on people. That is something that I have tried to harness all of my life, but you have unleashed the beast inside of me and I hate you for that too."

"Most people wouldn't have the stomach to do what I've done to you...what you did to my sister," I said, quietly kneeling down beside the bed so that we were at eye-level. "But...it doesn't bother me. And you know what? That's the part that scares me the most. Torturing you like this does not bother me one...little...bit. What I struggled with was the morality of it all. But, I'm ok with that now. The bible says an eye for an eye and a tooth for a tooth, and the way I figure after I'm finished with you...we'll be just about even."

Without warning, I jumped to my feet and swung that bat like a MLB professional, landing a skull-crushing blow right in the center of his forehead. The audible cracking sound it made gave me goose bumps. "Did you like that?" I asked sarcastically. I secured my footing and brought the bat back into position, swinging wildly blow after blow. I bashed Styler's head in with reckless abandon.

Finally, I stopped swinging. Only when I had completely exhausted myself did I see the extent of the damage I had done. Ross Styler was no more. All that was left of what had been his head was a bloody pile of skin, bone fragments, and hair. The sight of it made me vomit in spite of myself.

Due to the fact that I didn't have the luxury of time on my side, I couldn't afford to sit there nursing my stomach. After forcing myself to get up, I began gathering any evidence that I had ever been in the house.

It took about two hours, but I had finally removed all of the utensils, the generator, and lights.

When I was sure that I had gotten everything, I wiped down anything that I thought I might have touched including the bedposts. When that was finished, I vacuumed the floor, with a hand vacuum I had purchased for the occasion, in an attempt to suck up any telltale fibers of hair I may have lost. Once I was satisfied that everything was in order, I walked out of the basement and up the cellar stairs for the last time and did not look back. Styler was now a thing of the past and I had evidence to dispose of.

I knew eventually Styler's body would be discovered, but by that time any evidence that may have been overlooked would be long gone. Or so I hoped. But then again, it really didn't matter. I had accomplished what I had set out to do and that was all that mattered to me.

Chapter 22

My mouth was so dry that when I finally remembered to swallow, it felt as if I had been sucking on cotton balls. I pressed the stop button on my tape recorder and allowed the weight of the story I'd just heard to sink into my brain.

The only word that could be used to describe how I felt at that moment was "shocked". What I had just heard was nothing short of mind blowing, to say the least. "This woman is out of her rabbit mind!" I thought to myself. We sat in an awkward silence with her staring at me and me trying to avoid making any eye contact.

"I know that what I just told you is a little hard to take in," she began, "I know that what I did is very hard for you to understand. Please understand, Ms. Jackson, I'm not proud of what I did, and I hope that's not the impression I've given you. Please, say something. I want you to say whatever is on your mind."

I sat silently for a moment, weighing my thoughts very carefully before I spoke. "Ms. Langston, I really don't know how to process what you've just told me. I have to admit that I find it all very unsettling, but I sincerely hope that by the time we have finished, you will have found whatever it is you were searching for in asking me to come here."

"Me too," she said simply.

After the guards escorted Dawn from the room, I exited and made the long journey back to my car. Once on the road, I took out my cell phone and dialed Yolanda's number.

"Jackson!" she greeted enthusiastically, "What's the good word?"

"I just wanted to check in and let you know that I should have this all wrapped up by next week," I said dryly.

"You alright?"

"Right as rain."

"Ok, then. I'll look to have that story on my desk no later than midnight next Friday," she said. "Oh, and Jackson before I let you go…"

"Yeah?"

"Thanks for pulling this one out. I knew I could count on you." And before I could respond she hung up. Yolanda had never been one for sentiment, so I wasn't surprised.

I didn't feel like being alone with my thoughts at my apartment, so I decided to go visit my mother. My parents were always happy to receive a visit from their only child. But this time, I think I was more enamored with our reunion than they were.

When I saw my mother, I hugged her fiercely and kissed her cheek. "Vanessa, baby, is everything ok?" she asked, with a concerned look on her pretty face.

"Everything is fine. I just missed you that's all. Where's daddy?"

"He ran to the store to pick up some more potatoes for dinner. Do you want to eat?" Before I could answer, she was off to the kitchen to grab a third place setting so that I could join them. Watching her dart to and fro made me smile to myself as I sat comfortably on a barstool at the counter.

"Vanessa, start the salad for me will you, baby?"

"Yeah, no problem," I replied, moving to the refrigerator to grab the ingredients I'd need to prepare one of my famous tossed salads. "Mom?"

"Yeah, baby?"

"Have you ever wondered if you could take the life of another human being?" I asked.

Stopping in the middle of seasoning her chicken, she stared questioningly at me. "Why would you ask that?"

"It's this new assignment I'm on. I'm interviewing a woman that murdered the man who was the prime suspect in her sister's murder, but he got off on a technicality. So she kidnapped, tortured, and killed him and then turned herself in."

"My goodness, Vanessa, for the life of me I don't understand why you keep taking on these crazy assignments! I really worry about you spending so much time up there at that prison," she chastised.

"Mom, please. Can you just answer the question?"

"That's not an easy question to answer," she admitted, "I guess if someone did something to hurt my family then the thought might cross my mind. But thinking about it and actually doing it are obviously two very different things. Why are you asking me this question?"

"Because, I guess I'm trying to rationalize my own feelings about the situation. I mean…I've been listening to this woman's story and on one hand, I can identify with the hurt and anger she felt when her sister was murdered. God knows how devastated I would be if something like that ever happened to you or daddy. On the other hand...I know that it's not for us to take the law into our own hands. But if you only could have seen the pictures and heard her tell about the things he did to her sister and all those other people, and the things he said... I just don't understand how the justice system could allow someone so evil, and obviously guilty, to just slip through the cracks! I mean, it's almost like, if the court would have done what it was supposed to do, then she never would've been able to do what she did. Does that make sense?"

My mother looked at me thoughtfully as she continued to rub seasoning on her chicken, and then smiled slightly. "It sounds to me like you're afraid that you might be starting to agree with what this woman did, and you want to justify it by blaming the justice system. Is that correct?" she asked, pointedly allowing the attorney in her to surface.

"I don't know," I stated honestly. "I know that what she did was wrong, but if you could have heard her tell her story..."

"Look, baby, I work for the legal system so I understand all too well how perfectly flawed it is. But be that as it may," she explained, "that is still not an excuse to take the law into your own hands. If people aren't held accountable for what they do, then this society would become an open free-for-all and nobody would be safe. There has to be order.

"Now," she went on to say, "that's not to say that if someone were to do to my baby girl what was done to that woman's sister, that I wouldn't want to blow the head off the bastard that did it! I believe that's just human nature to want to protect the people you love and to lash out at those who seek to harm them. Did I answer your question?"

"Yes, mom, you did. Thank you."

"Good," she replied, waving her hand to dismiss the subject. "That's enough talk about depressing stuff. Now hurry up with that salad so we can try to have dinner ready by the time your daddy gets back."

Chapter 23

The funny thing about time is that it never seems to move the way you want it to. When you're looking forward to something, it never moves fast enough. But when you're dreading something, it always seems to fly. So needless to say, I wasn't surprised when I found myself back in the visitor's chamber at the prison waiting for Dawn Langston to make her grand entrance once again.

When she finally arrived, I felt a strange sense of anticipation as I patiently waited for the guards to secure her restraints. Now that we had gotten through the gruesome details of the how and why, I wanted to hear about the consequences and repercussions. I had been struggling with a tremendous amount of inner turmoil since our last visit. And I wasn't quite sure if I was ready to hear the rest of the story, even though I couldn't imagine the conclusion being any worse than what I had already heard.

She admitted to methodically kidnapping, torturing, and killing Styler, but that I already knew. I was anxious to hear about why she turned herself in, if she wasn't sorry about what she had done.

Once she was situated, I didn't waste any time getting straight to the punch. "Good morning, Ms. Langston. At the conclusion of our last meeting, you told about the kidnap, torture, and murder of Ross Styler. It is my hope that by the conclusion of today's session that we'll be able to complete the interview in its entirety."

"That shouldn't be a problem."

"Good."

"I scare you, don't I?" she asked pointedly.

"No, Ms. Langston, you don't scare me, I am trying to understand you," I stated honestly, "I am trying to understand how someone that seems so normal could do the things that you did and not have any qualms about it. I mean, don't get me wrong...I feel for you and the loss you suffered. But that still doesn't change the fact that you took it upon yourself to not just kill a man, but you tortured him. I fathom how you went through with it. So do you scare me? No. Do you unsettle me? Yes."

"Fair enough," she said, "I sincerely hope that by the end of our time together you gain some kind of closure about that, Ms. Washington. Really I do. But I guess in the grand scheme of things, I really don't need for you to understand it...I just need for you to tell about it. That is why they call you the 'voice', isn't it?"

I was visibly shaken by her callousness, but all in all she was right. All I had to do was tell the story- nothing more, nothing less. Even though I was extremely irritated by what she had just said to me, I managed to push my feelings aside so I could finish what I'd come there to do.

Placing my recorder on the table, I pressed the button and folded my hands. "So tell me what happened after the night of the murder?"

Chapter 24

I woke up the following Saturday morning to the sun shining brightly on my face. I opened my eyes and marveled at how well I had slept the night before. I hadn't felt that rested in over three years.

As I moved to get out of bed, my body screamed out in pain reminding me of the previous night's activities. After swinging the bat full throttle as many times as I did, then hauling the generator and all the other equipment out of the house, and then pulling it out of the car again to dump it in the junk yard I'd found, my back, arms, and legs were extremely sore. I was never one to complain about aches and pains that resulted from a good work out, so I just had to grit my teeth and push through the discomfort so that I could get on with my day. After all, I had a date with Chris and I was not about to cancel it.

It was almost eleven o'clock when I finally got into the shower, so I didn't spend as much time as I would have liked allowing the hot water to massage my aching muscles. After hopping out, I bumped my hair with a few curls, threw on a cute little sundress with matching sandals, and I was ready to go. I had to admit, as I gave myself a once-over in the mirror, that even though I had always considered myself a bonafide tomboy, I cleaned up pretty well.

I had pinned my hair up and allowed a few strands to elegantly accentuate my neck, while my dress showed off my athletically chiseled arms and complimented my nicely shaped legs. Even though I was muscularly defined from my intense workouts, I still managed to maintain my femininity. I was toned and cut without appearing bulky, which I was thankful for because the last thing I wanted to do was scare Chris off because my arms were bigger than his.

Twelve 'o clock couldn't come fast enough for me. When he finally rang my buzzer, I had to stop myself from running downstairs to meet him. "Calm down," I told myself. When I finally made it to the front door, he was standing there waiting patiently, looking just as handsome as ever.

"Hey, gorgeous," he said taking my hand and kissing me softly on the cheek.

"Hello. How are you today?"

"I can't complain. Definitely better now that I'm here with you."

Even though I knew it was a line he had probably said a thousand times before to a thousand different girls, I still blushed in spite of myself. I couldn't remember the last time I had felt this giddy with a man. Just a touch of his hand was enough to make my heart race. The more I thought about it, the more I realized that I couldn't remember it because it had never happened.

"So, where are we going?"

"It's a surprise."

"I don't like surprises."

"You'll like this one."

"No, you need to tell me where we're going first. I don't like surprises! What if I'm over dressed? I don't dress like this for everything."

He laughed and pulled me so close that his lips were only inches from my ear. "You are not over dressed," he whispered, "and I promise that you are going to love the surprise. Do you trust me?"

"I don't know..."

"Do you trust me?" he asked again, his blue eyes sparkling mischievously.

At that moment all I wanted to do was be close to him, so I put all my reservations aside and got into the car. After a forty-five minute drive to Auburn Hills, we arrived at an oriental novelty store that I had never heard of. He parked the car, turned off the engine, and then turned to me with a smirk on his face.

"Ok, I know that you have some serious control issues, but if I'm going to do this you have to trust me. Ok?"

I looked around the parking lot, which was fairly crowded, so I concluded that he wasn't going to do anything too crazy in broad daylight. So, I decided to play along. "Ok," I replied.

"Ok. Now, since this is a surprise, I'm going to put a blindfold over your eyes and then I will come around and get you out of the car. Then I'm going to lead you into the store. Once we're inside you have to leave the blindfold on until I tell you to take it off. Ok?"

"Ok!"

"You have to promise."

"Ok, I promise! Let's just do it before I change my mind!" I laughed.

He pulled a bandana out of his pocket and tied it securely over my eyes. Then he helped me out of the car and led me into the store. I had goose pimples all over my arms because I was so nervous. He was right. I had serious control issues and did not like to be surprised. But, since he had obviously gone through a lot of trouble to put everything together, I figured I owed it to him to play along.

After standing blindfolded in the front of a strange place for what seemed like forever, I began to get irritated. "Chris, what is taking so long? I'm taking this blindfold off now! What are you doing?"

"No! Don't take it off yet! It'll only take a few more seconds," he promised. "Now hold your hands out."

I hesitantly extended both of my arms with my palms facing up. I soon felt a cold piece of smooth metal in my hands. I wrapped my fingers around it to see if I could tell what it might be but I knew it couldn't possibly be what I thought it was.

"Go ahead, open your eyes," he said.

Snatching the blindfold off, I laid my eyes upon the most beautiful handcrafted Japanese sword I had ever seen. I had practiced with swords in my training but never with an instrument as exquisitely made as the one I now held. The sword itself was approximately three feet long, with an engraved stainless steel blade that was two and a half feet. The handle was expertly crafted from the finest Japanese leather. I was speechless.

"Well, what are you waiting for? Try it out."

"I…I can't accept this."

"Please, I know you love martial arts and I remember you telling me that you loved the ancient art of sword fighting. Well, now you have your own sword. Just please…don't hurt anybody with that," he laughed.

"If he only knew," I thought to myself.

"My friend owns this store, so he gave me a really good deal on it. I saw it when I was out here a few days ago and I had to get it for you. I hope you'll accept it."

"I don't know what to say, Chris. I love it," I said, genuinely touched, "thank you."

The rest of the day was a blur because it went by so fast. Before I knew it, nightfall had come around and we decided to go downtown to Campus Martius so we could sit in the park.

"Can I ask you something?" he asked.

"Yeah."

"How have you been doing? I mean really?"

"What do you mean?"

"I mean, I've been wondering how you've really been doing, since the death of your sister?"

"What would make you ask me that?" I asked evenly.

"I see it all the time in my line of work. People deal with tragedy in a lot of different ways. But you… you haven't dealt with it in any of the typical ways that I'm used to seeing. So, I just want to make sure that you're ok."

I looked at him thoughtfully for a moment. Where was this coming from all of a sudden? Why would he ask me something like that out of the blue?

The look on his face said that he was genuinely asking out of concern, but the knot in my stomach urged me to be very cautious.

"I just take it day by day," I admitted, choosing my words very carefully, "I can't say that I'm over it because I'm not. I still don't understand how he could get off like that, but I guess I have no choice but to accept it and move on with my life. I miss my sister so much it hurts sometimes, but I feel like I have to stay strong for my family. My parents don't seem to be fairing as well."

"I would love to meet them…under normal circumstances that is," he said smiling.

"Maybe one day you will," I teased.

The rest of the evening continued just as smoothly as all of our other dates. Chris was so easy to be with that I almost forgot about what I had done the night before, until a phone call ended our date abruptly.

"I have to get down to the station," he stated, after hanging up, "I'm sorry, but something major just came up and I have to get to a crime scene."

"Ok. What happened?"

"I can't talk about it right now, but don't you worry I'll call you tomorrow. Everything will be fine. It's all just part of the job," he explained, as he took me by the hand and walked me back to his car.

The conversation on the way back to my apartment was minimal, partly due to the fact that he was on the phone with his office trying to get whatever pertinent information he needed. I on the other hand, was lost in my thoughts. I silently wondered if the crime scene he spoke of had anything to do with the little present I had left for Ross Styler's brother. Glancing at him from the corner of my eye, I marveled at how his whole demeanor had changed within a matter of moments. He was in full detective mode, with his eyes hardened and jaw tightly clenched. I knew that whatever the case was he was being called in for, he was the type of man who would not rest until it was solved. I just hoped that this particular case wouldn't be something that would lead him back to me.

Chapter 25

After Chris dropped me off, I decided to go straight to bed. The last thing I needed to do was drive myself crazy wondering about the crime scene call he'd received. After all, this was Detroit and crime wasn't something that didn't happen on a regular basis.

Before I turning in for the night, I decided to call my mother to check in and let her know everything had gone well on my date. Needless to say, she was very talkative at that point wanting to know every minute detail about my evening with Detective Jones, and when I was bringing him over there to have dinner with her and daddy.

"Mom, please, not tonight. I just wanted to call and let you know I was ok, so you wouldn't worry."

"Ok, baby. Just give me a call tomorrow if you get a chance. Goodnight."

"Goodnight," I replied, hanging up with a sigh. I had a feeling that I was going to be in for a long night.

Fortunately, I was finally able to fall asleep and the next morning I was faced with the ordeal of having to go back to work on Monday. Needless to say, that after committing murder, punching a clock hardly seemed to be anything of earth shattering importance in the grand scheme of things.

Aggravated at the mere thought of having to go back to work, I decided I needed to thoroughly enjoy my Sunday. I figured I would treat myself to a day of lounging around the house and get caught up on the rest I didn't get, when I was supposed to be on vacation.

Just as I was settling into my favorite spot on the couch to dive into a book, the phone rang.

"Hello."

"Hello there, gorgeous. Did you sleep well last night?" Chris's sexy voice drifted through my receiver.

"As well as can be expected when my perfect night ended so abruptly, leaving me to spend the rest of my night alone."

"I'll make it up to you, I promise. But in the mean time, I have something that I need to talk to you about. Can you meet me at Ram's Horn on Telegraph?"

"Yeah, sure. Is everything ok?" I asked nervously.

"I'm not sure, but I'll talk to you about it when I see you. Meet me there at one, ok?"

"Ok." My heart began to race as I hung up the phone. He had to know about Styler. "What else could it be?" I wondered.

I couldn't afford to get worked up about this. All I had to do was coach myself through it and everything would be fine. I had covered my tracks thoroughly, so the only way anyone would know anything would be if I panicked and did something stupid. All I had to do was be cool.

So that's what I did. When I arrived at the restaurant, Chris was already seated in a booth waiting for me. He stood and greeted me with a hug and kiss on the cheek before I slid into the seat on the opposite side.

"Thanks for coming down here on such short notice."

"It's ok. So what's up, Chris?" I said, feigning concern.

"You know the crime scene I got called to last night?" He paused and I nodded my head, "Well apparently, somebody sent Nico Styler a little present that included two of his brother's fingers. Do you know who Nico Styler is?"

"Isn't he the brother of the man who killed my sister?"

"Right. Ross Styler has been missing since Monday, and this is the first break I've gotten since he disappeared."

"How do you know he's been missing since Monday?"

He looked around cautiously and then met my eyes with a fixed gaze. "I've been following him since he was acquitted. Keeping tabs and gathering evidence for the next time he slips up. But now that this has happened, I can open a new case and really dig in to see what this guy has really been up to. I'm sure that it's some kind of drug related retaliation or something, but I'm still going to do some digging to see what I can come up with."

I paced my response by slowly allowing my face to arrange itself into a look of surprise when he finished his statement. After I had allowed our silence to become uncomfortable, I spoke. "Why didn't you tell me?"

"I couldn't tell you because I wasn't supposed to be doing it. If my superiors found out that I've been following an acquitted suspect around for the past three years, I'd be in a lot of trouble."

"So why are you telling me this now?"

"Because I feel like I owe you that much. I saw how hard you took the death of your sister and I know you feel like the system is a joke, so I just wanted you to know that some of us do take our jobs very seriously." At that moment, I felt a pang of guilt because here he was putting his job on the line for me and I was lying to him.

"Dawn," he continued, "I am treading in some very deep waters right now because I really like you. I've been feeling you since the day I met you, and now that I've gotten to know you, it's only getting stronger. I don't want you to hurt anymore. So, I'm going to see this thing through to the end, so that hopefully you and your family can finally have some closure."

Somehow I managed to maintain a straight face, but inside my conscience was tearing me apart. Though I took great solace in the fact that Ross Styler had died by my hand, I didn't enjoy lying to Chis. One thing was for sure, guilt or no guilt, I had to pull myself together or I was going to prison.

Chapter 26

As the days went on, the weeks turned into months and I tried to forget about Ross Styler, and for a while it seemed like all of my problems had all but disappeared. Chris and I continued to date and things were progressing very nicely. You could even say that they were getting pretty serious.

I had finally taken him to see my parents and they hit it off immediately. He and my dad bonded over beer and talks of politics and how the whole government seemed to be going to hell in a hand basket in the hands of Bush. My mom embraced him for the simple fact that she felt like anybody who could hold my attention for more than a week, had to be pretty special.

As hard as I tried to pace myself and keep in mind that Chris could very well be the key to my undoing, I couldn't deny that I was falling in love with him. The more time we spent together, the harder it was for me to be away from him. We could talk for hours on end about everything and nothing all at the same time, or just sit in comfortable silence. His wisdom and outlook on life always proved to be a welcomed challenge for my natural defiance of everything, and after we were done debating we would succumb to long stretches of lovemaking. Everything about him was strong, noble, and honest. He was everything that I could ever want in a man. Deep down inside, I knew that I didn't deserve to be with someone like him.

Though he had stopped talking to me about work, I always found myself wondering if he was making any progress with the Styler case. Almost three months had gone by and they still hadn't found the body. I felt that the likelihood of anyone finding it would be slim to none. Nine times out of ten, that house was going to be condemned sooner or later since so many new homes were going up in the area.

I had become very complacent with my life for the first time in a very long while. But no sooner had I let my guard down than karma came back to bite me in the ass.

"Nico Styler has put out a fifty thousand dollar reward for information leading to whoever killed his brother," Chris said one day.

"How do you know he was killed?" I asked, "Did somebody find a body?"

"No, not yet, but we're pretty sure he's dead after being gone this long."

"I can't say I'm sorry to hear that," I said, before I could stop myself. Chris looked at me briefly but said nothing. I bit my lip and silently cursed myself for being so careless.

"Well, this is definitely going to stir up some activity on this case. Now we'll have every crackhead, hoodrat, and snitch calling the station cooking up half-baked stories, just to see if they can get a chance at getting that money."

"You never know, something might turn up."

"Yeah, maybe. So let me ask you something," he said pointedly, "what do you think about all this?"

"What do you mean?"

"I mean, the man that killed your sister has turned up missing, and for all practical purposes is probably dead. How does that make you feel?"

"I just said that I'm not sorry to hear that."

"I know, but you're not answering the question."

"I don't know, Chris!" I said heatedly, "What do you want me to say? Nothing would make me happier than to see that bastard laid out on a cold slab of metal with his dick shoved down his throat! Is that what you wanted to hear me say?"

"I want you to express some sort of feelings about it! Ever since I told you about the situation with the severed fingers being sent to Nico Styler's club, you haven't asked any questions about the case or anything else. That's not normal, Dawn."

"Oh, so now you think you know what's normal for me?"

"The man killed your sister! Your sister!" he shot back. "You are keeping everything bottled up and it's not healthy, you gotta deal with your hatred toward this man somehow or it's going to eat you alive. I saw how you reacted in that courtroom...you had murder in your eyes. And now I'm sitting here telling you that he may be dead and you don't react one way or the other. I need for you to open up and talk to me."

"Look, Chris, I'm not going to sit here and let you psychoanalyze me. How I deal with my problems is my business. Have you ever lost a sister? Have you?"

"No," he said reluctantly.

"Then don't sit there and try to tell me how I'm supposed to be acting. I hate Ross Styler! I hate him with every bone in my body and I pray to God every night that his soul rots in hell! If somebody did kill that sick bastard, then I would like nothing better than to meet that lucky bastard, shake his hand, and offer him my first born child as a gift of gratitude. Is that what you wanted to hear, Chris?"

"Yes," he said walking over to gather me into his arms, "that's exactly what I needed to hear, baby. I need to know that you're dealing with this. You can't keep your feelings bottled up, Dawn. That kind of stuff will tear you up inside. Believe me, I know. I've been doing this job for a long time and I've seen hatred do some evil things to the best of men. You gotta know that you can't always deal with everything on your own."

Though I desperately fought it, the floodgates opened and brought forth a tirade of tears that I didn't know existed. I cried like I wanted to cry when I first saw my sister's dead body in the morgue, how I wanted to cry when her casket was lowered into the ground but couldn't because the searing hot rage inside of me wouldn't allow it. Right then and there in the arms of the man I loved, I let it go. I let it all go and it felt good. I cried for my mother, I cried for my father, and finally I cried for me. I had avenged my sister's death and now I had earned the right to have my emotional breakdown. Lord knew I needed it.

"It's ok, baby," he said, as he softly stroked my back, "I'm here. Everything's going to be ok, I promise."

Chapter 27

Sometimes Murphy's Law is a big monster of a pain in the ass. Not only did Nico Styler's fifty thousand dollar reward stir up a big commotion around the disappearance of Ross Styler, but it seemed like from the time that Chris told me about the reward money my luck just got worse and worse.

For starters, one night some nosy little teenagers decided to go into my old hideout for kicks to do some exploring. They broke a window and went in through the side kitchen door. I can only assume that during their investigations they ventured to the basement, where they must have been hit by the stench of Styler's rotting flesh in the cellar below. Needless to say, they found the body and the police were called out to the scene. Since the Detroit Police Department had headed up the previous investigation, the Romulus Police Department called them in to assist with the case.

When Chris got the news, he almost beat the Romulus police to the scene. He called me immediately to let me know he was on his way out there. Once he arrived, he assured me that he would call as soon as he could with an update. My heart dropped into my stomach when I hung up the phone.

"What am I going to do now?" I asked myself out loud. After a few minutes of mulling it over, I decided that there was no use stressing myself out about it because ultimately, whatever was going to happen would happen. So with that thought in mind, I went to work just like I would any other day.

After work I went to sparring practice so I could work off some nervous energy, and by the time I got home I was exhausted. I checked my messages to see if Chris had called and he hadn't. It was after seven and usually we would have talked at least twice by now. I pushed the nagging feeling of guilt from my mind and told myself that he was doing his job and would call me when he got a chance.

Since relaxing was completely out of the question, I went to my parents' house so I could try to take my mind off what was going on at the crime scene. Fortunately, my mother was in one of her rare chipper moods and wanted me to go shopping with her.

We returned from the mall around nine-thirty and I still couldn't understand why I hadn't heard from Chris, so after I dropped my mother off I headed home. Unable to stand it any longer, I dialed Chris's cell phone number and it went straight to voicemail. "Damnit!" I swore throwing my phone down on the passenger seat.

Two days later, I still hadn't heard from Chris and I was really starting to worry, so on my way home from work I called his job to make sure that he was still alive. The receptionist, or whoever it was that answered the phone, assured me that he was fine and she would be sure to let him know that I had called.

After I ascertained that he hadn't been killed in the line of duty, I immediately switched gears from worried to pissed off mode. I didn't care if he was working on a case or not, it didn't take but a minute to pick up the phone to call and let someone know that you were ok.

By the time I pulled into my parking lot thirty minutes later, I was so lost in my thoughts that I walked right by Chris's parked car. Just as I was about to insert my key into the front door, a hand reached out and touched my shoulder.

I immediately swung around ready to pounce, but when I saw that it was him I relaxed. "What are you doing? You almost got your ass kicked," I said angrily.

"We need to talk," he replied seriously.

"About what? What's wrong?"

"Please, let's just go inside so we can talk."

Taking note of the seriousness in his tone, I opened the door and led him upstairs to my apartment. I didn't want to appear nervous, so I busied myself with preparing drinks for us to sip on while we talked.

"Can you sit down for a minute? I need to look you in the eye when we have this conversation." His words halted my movement and caused my heart to jump into my throat. I couldn't imagine what could have happened over the past couple of days that would warrant his current disposition, but I knew that whatever it was, it wasn't good.

Swallowing the huge lump that had formed in my throat, I sat down at the table and looked him squarely in the eye. His five o'clock shadow made him look haggard and worn, and his eyes were red from lack of sleep. He paced back and forth across the room as if trying to weigh the words he was about to speak, and then finally sat down in the chair next to me.

"What we found in the basement of that house was very disturbing to say the least," he began, "I won't go into detail about what was done to the body, but it was pretty bad. My squad combed over that crime scene with a fine tooth comb and they weren't able to come up with a whole lot…"

My pulse raced as I waited for him to continue. "Then on my way out, I decided to take one last look around the parameter, and that's when I noticed a set of partial tire tracks off to the side. They stuck out because all of the squad cars were parked in the same vicinity in front of the house, so I asked some of the other officers if anyone else had driven around back for any reason and they said no. I went back out and examined the tracks and saw that they weren't fresh and they were in a spot where there were patches of grass and dirt. I don't know how old they were, but for some reason the dirt held the imprint of those tracks."

"Anyway, I called one of my forensic guys to come down and take some photos and sneak a mold out of it to take back to our lab to be analyzed. I had an idea of what kind of car the tracks belonged to just by looking at them, but I wanted to be sure before I said anything," he said, looking at me pointedly. "I got the results back this morning, and tread from those tires came from a fifteen inch wheel on a mid-sized vehicle."

It took a massive concentrated effort for me to maintain a neutral facial expression, but somehow I managed to hold his gaze without flinching. "And what does this have to do with me and why I haven't heard from you in the past two days, Chris?"

"Dawn, don't play games with me. I'm a detective and this is what I do. You drive a mid-sized vehicle with fifteen-inch wheels, you live in Inkster which is only a ten minute drive from where the body was found, and judging from what was done to the body, it would appear that someone reenacted the scene from your sister's murder. And I'm willing to bet that if I was to go outside right now and take pictures of your tires, the tread will match what I have at my lab. Am I right?"

I could feel my blood beginning to boil as I tried to maintain my composure. I couldn't believe that this was happening. I knew I was playing a dangerous game by getting involved with him, but I never dreamed it would turn out this way. I didn't trust myself to speak at that moment, so I said nothing.

"Damnit!" he yelled, striking the table with his fist and jumping up. He began pacing back and forth, his anger rising by the second. "Why? Why did you do it?"

"I didn't..." I began in an attempt to defend myself.

"Don't fucking lie to me! Do you know what this means? Dawn, you are going to prison for the rest of your natural life! Do you realize that?"

The hurt look on his face told me that there was no need in trying to keep up the charade of pleading my innocence, so I decided to level with him. I felt I owed him that much. "Yes," I said calmly, "I realized that from the moment I decided to kill him. The justice system failed and I corrected their error, end of story."

"Baby, it doesn't work like that," he said, sitting back down and burying his head in his hands. "Look, we gotta figure something out. The results came back this morning, but I told my guy to keep it under wraps until I could check some things out first. That will buy us some time. I gotta figure out how to fix this..."

"Wait a minute!" I said, "What do you mean figure something out?"

"Dawn, I can't let you go to prison," he looked up with pain in his eyes, "I love you."

Tears immediately sprang to my eyes. I was torn. I couldn't believe that he was willing to break the law to keep me from going to prison. It went against everything that he stood for and I couldn't let him do it.

"I love you too, Chris," I said, kneeling in front of him. "I love you for everything you did to try to bring Carmen's killer to justice. I love you for waking me up inside, and I love you for loving me enough to forsake everything that you stand for to keep me out of prison. But, I can't let you do that. I won't let you do it." I kissed his hands as tears coursed down my cheeks.

"Let's not talk about it anymore tonight. Let's just go to bed and we'll deal with this in the morning, ok?" I kissed him gently urging him to meet my need to have him close to me. Though he resisted at first, soon we were passionately clinging to each other, kissing as if our lives depended on it.

Before long, he picked me up and carried me to my bedroom, leaving a trail of clothing in our wake. We made love for hours on end until finally, we both passed out from exhaustion, tightly embraced in each other's arms.

The next morning, I opened my eyes as the sun peaked through my window. I turned and stroked

Chris's sleeping face and marveled at how peaceful he looked. Slipping silently out of bed, I pulled my clothes on and sat on the edge staring at him for the longest time. I knew what I had to do, I just didn't know how I was going to tell him or my parents about my decision. Finally, after pondering it over and over, I kissed him softly and left my apartment for the last time to go do what I had to do before I lost the nerve.

Chapter 28

After I pulling into the parking lot of the Romulus police station, I sat in my car for another thirty minutes weighing my options. If I turned myself in, I was going to spend the rest of my life behind bars. My parents would have to suffer the loss of another child and I would have to be without Chris.

If I didn't turn myself in, he could possibly lose his job for tampering with evidence and I would more than likely have to spend the rest of my life on the run. Either way, my parents would still be devastated.

"Carmen," I said out loud, "I know you can hear me. I miss you so much! I don't know how everything got so crazy, but my temper has gotten me in trouble again. Only this time daddy can't pay a medical bill and make it all go away."

"Now I'm sitting here outside this police station trying to decide if I should do the easy thing or the right thing." I was silent for a moment as I allowed the sun to caress my face. I knew I wasn't crazy, but I felt Carmen's love in the warmth of those rays and it brought a feeling of peace over me. "I know, I just needed to hear it out loud. I love you, sis, and I hope you can understand why I did what I did. I don't care what anybody says, he deserved it. But, Chris doesn't deserve to suffer for me and neither does mommy or daddy. So, if you get a chance, please ask God to forgive me. Maybe one day, I'll get to the point where I'll be sorry and then I'll feel ok about asking him myself."

Just as I was about to get out of the car, my cell phone rang. I knew who it was before I checked the caller ID, but I stared at the number anyway. After debating on whether or not to answer, I finally picked it up on the fourth ring. "Hello."

"Don't do it," Chris said, "I can make this work, Dawn. All I have to do is put them on a wild goose chase with some other cars and we'll go get new tires for your car. It's as simple as that. No one will ever know."

"Chris, I love you," I said with tears streaming down my face, "you just make sure that you come and visit me sometime."

Without another word, I hung up the phone, got out of the car, walked into the police station, and turned myself in. There really wasn't a lot of ruckus around my confession like I thought there would be, the RPD officers were efficient, professional, and surprisingly nice to me.

They read me my rights and after I waived my right to an attorney, they took my full confession. I told them about how Ross Styler had murdered my sister three years prior and got off on a technicality, and then I proceeded to tell them in detail about how I methodically planned and carried out his kidnap, torture, and murder. After it was all said and done, I was allowed to make one phone call which turned out to be the hardest call I've ever had to make.

"Hello," my mother's voice drifted through the phone.

"Hi, mom."

"Dawn, why are you calling here from a restricted number? Is everything ok?"

"No, mommy, everything is not ok..." Then I proceeded to reiterate the same story to her that I had just told the police.

After I was finished, my mother cried hysterically and assured me that she and my father would do everything they could to get me the best attorney they could afford. "Don't you worry, baby," she choked, "your dad and I will be up there as soon as possible. You just sit tight. I'm not going to let them keep you in there!"

"I'm ok, mom. They're taking good care of me here, so don't worry. I just wanted you to hear this from me and not find out from the news. Please don't come here. I love you, mommy," I said, "and please tell daddy that I love him too."

After speaking with my mom, I felt like I was ready for anything from that point on. I was ready to accept full responsibility for what I had done, so come what may.

When it finally did come, it came like a landslide. The story hit the news that Ross Styler's killer had turned herself in and the media was on it like white on rice. They invaded the Romulus station like rodents. It caused such a ruckus that I had to be secretly transported to Wayne County.

After hours of waiting and running around, my parents were finally able to find out where I was so that they could come to see me. When they came to let me know that I had visitors, I was reluctant to come out but then decided not to put them through any additional heartache.

When I entered the visiting room, my mother immediately began to cry when she saw me in my jail issued gear and handcuffs, while my father tried to maintain his composure.

"Dawn, we are going to get you out of here," my mother said indignantly, "We hired an attorney and you'll be out of here in no time."

"Mom, please…"

"No, honey, you'll be home before…"

"Mother!" I yelled. "Stop it! I'm not getting out of here. I killed a man and I am going to be in here for a very long time. I know that and you're going to have to accept it too. I don't want you wasting money on no high priced attorney."

"Dawn, be reasonable," my dad asserted, "this lawyer might be able to do something to help you out of this. Just let us help you."

"Daddy, I know what I did and I know that what I did was wrong. I've already signed a full confession. End of story. There is nothing more to do or say."

"But that man deserved to die!" my mother blurted out. "He killed my baby and they let him get away with it and now they want to let you sit in here and rot because you did something about it!"

"Calm down, baby," my dad said attempting to soothe my mother.

"Don't you tell me to calm down! They're trying to take another child away from me and I won't let them, William! Do you hear me?" she screamed.

At that point, the guards came and escorted my parents out and I was led back to my cell. For the next two weeks, my mother continued to send the attorney but every time he came, I refused to see him. Finally she got the picture and the attorney stopped coming, even though she and my father came faithfully every other day.

The next time the guards informed me that I had a visitor, I automatically assumed it was one of my parents but received a pleasant surprise when I saw Chris sitting on the other side of the glass. A lump immediately jumped into my throat as I sat down and held the phone to my ear.

"Hi," I said.

"Hey, gorgeous," he replied, "how you holding up in here?"

"You know me. I haven't had any problems yet. I'm sure it won't be so easy going when I make my move to the big house," I said lightly, "but I'll make sure that they only try me once."

"That's my girl," he said cracking a smile.

"So what took you so long?"

"Couldn't bear to see you like this. Why are you refusing legal counsel?"

"I don't want my parents spending money they don't have trying to get me out of here."

"I'll pay for it."

"Stop it."

"Why are you making this so hard?" he asked angrily.

"Chris, I'm sorry that this is so hard for you! I am accepting the consequences of what I did. I turned myself in because it was the right thing to do and you know it! I am not sorry about what I did, and if I would have walked away and let you do what you were planning to do, I wouldn't have been any better than Ross Styler."

His knuckles turned white as he gripped the phone, yet he said nothing.

"Baby, I killed a white man. You know as well as I do, that even in Detroit, that isn't going to ride. Your justice system is not built for people who look like me, that's why I had to do what I did. Maybe one day, I'll walk out of here but for now I just want to get this thing over with as soon a possible."

"Fine," he said standing to leave, "if that's what you want then so be it."

After he left, I went back to my cell and went to sleep. I stayed in that facility for about two months to await sentencing. When my case finally went before the judge there was no jury and no debating. I was sentenced to two consecutive life sentences without the possibility of parole for first-degree manslaughter and one count of kidnapping. No muss no fuss, just lock the door and throw away the key.

Chapter 29

"Now here it is four years later and here I am, sitting here sharing my story with the Women's Lib Magazine," she concluded. "So, what do you think, Ms. Jackson? Do you think I'm crazy?"

I had to admit that her story had blown my mind. I was completely at a loss for words. As I sat there fidgeting with my recorder, I tried to imagine Detective Jones, and found myself wondering where he was now in relation to all of this.

"What happed to Detective Jones," I asked.

"He's still around. He writes and comes to visit me every now and then. We still love each other very much, but I try to encourage him to move on with his life. I want him to be happy even if we can't be together. He's a good man," she said.

"You mentioned that you had long hair at one point, when did you cut it?"

"When I first got here, I asked the people to chop it off. I don't need hair in here. It only serves as a hindrance when things get heated."

I looked her over while she sat in her restraints and weighed the information that she had just given me. "Why are you really in those restraints?" I asked.

"Ms. Jackson, prison is not a glamorous place by any stretch of your imagination. There are some very debaucherous people in here, and given my temperament and the fact that I murdered the brother of a very high profile drug dealer, sometimes it gets a little rough in here for me, if you know what I mean. Knowing this, I find that it's better for me to be alone so I'm not tempted to beat the shit out of people who insist on trying my patience," she explained. "Plus, from what I hear, Nico Styler has a hit out on me. No one can watch my back like I can, and unfortunately solitary confinement is the only option granted to us problem children."

"I see. So now that you have been in here for this long, do you feel any remorse for what you did yet?"

"No, can't say that I do. But I feel that God is working with me on that. Since I've been in here, I've found comfort in studying the bible. I understand the principles that it teaches and I'm learning to embrace them. I believe that in time I'll feel worthy enough to go to God in prayer and ask His forgiveness for what I did. But until I can have remorse in my heart, I don't feel like I have the right to ask God's forgiveness for something I'm not truly sorry for. Call it pride or whatever, but that's just how I feel about it. I just pray that I will be able to overcome that before it's too late. Do you think that's wrong?"

I contemplated her question for a moment and then responded, "I think that if you ask for forgiveness and mean it, then God will work out the rest. And you're right, it is pride. Once you let your pride go, I think that you'll notice a change in your life, Ms. Langston, and for the better. Your sister is gone and now so is her killer, and now you have to move on with your life. Hatred has brought you here, but who knows what might happen if you let it go."

"I don't presume to judge you, but you asked for my opinion and that's what I think," I said honestly.

Her eyes glistened, as she turned her face to the wall. "But what if I can't let it go?"

"Then you are probably going to die in here," I replied sadly. She continued to stare at the wall as I gathered my belongings and prepared to leave. My heart was no longer heavy because I had come to the conclusion that no matter what happened in life, there was always a choice. No matter what I heard on any of these assignments, or what I thought about the outcome of any of the situations, nothing could change me unless I allowed it to. So the fear I'd felt in taking on this project was completely unmitigated.

"Thank you for the interview, Ms. Langston. I'll be praying for you and I hope that you will do the same for me."

She smiled briefly and nodded her head as the guards came to escort her back to her cell. For me, it was back to the office and back to the grind. This was a story that had to be told and Yolanda was not going to wait too much longer to get it.

Chapter 30

"Well, Jackson, I have to say, you never fail to impress me," Yolanda stated after reading my unfinished piece on Dawn Langston for the fourth time. "I know I've said this twice before, but this has to be your best work yet!"

"Thank you," I replied dryly.

"Awww, come on now! It wasn't that bad was it? You learned a lot, didn't you?"

I smiled in spite of myself and nodded my head. "Yolanda, you have no idea what it's like to go into that place and sit with those women, reliving their tainted lives. It's mentally and emotionally draining."

"But you do it so well, Jackson! That's why you're my star! Look at all these awards," she said with a sweeping gesture to point out all of the various journalism plaques and certificates that decorated my walls. "You have a gift, Vanessa, and what you're doing for these women has never been done before. How many publications out there do you think would give an average person the time of day if it's not a national case? We are giving these women a chance to be heard and understood, and most importantly, we're giving them closure. Remember that." After the grand stand speech she had just made, she made an even more dramatic exit, leaving me alone with my thoughts.

There was only one thing missing from this project as far as my closure was concerned, and that was fact that I had not spoken to Detective Jones. For him to be willing to risk his job to keep her from going to prison, there had to be something in him that needed to be brought forth. Knowing myself the way I did, I wasn't going to be able to turn the project in until I had exhausted every possibility to get a chance to sit down and talk to him. So I went out on a limb and called his office.

As luck would have it, he answered his phone on the second ring. "Detective Jones, how may I help you?" His voice was sexy as hell over the phone."

"Hello, Detective Jones," I said catching myself, "my name is Vanessa Jackson and I am a reporter from the Women's Lib Magazine. The reason for my call is that, I just interviewed Dawn Langston, at her request, about her case. I was wondering if you would be willing to meet with me, so that I might get a clearer understanding on a few things."

After a moment of silence, he said, "Sure, I guess that would be ok. When do you want to meet?"

"Today if possible. I'm on deadline, and I'd like to turn this in as soon as possible."

"Ok then, you can meet me here in my office at three-thirty. Do you know where the 36th District Precinct is?"

"I sure do."

"Ok, I'll see you then." And with that he hung up.

I literally sat at my desk and counted down the minutes until it was time for me to meet with Detective Jones. When I finally arrived at his office, I sat nervously in the waiting room trying to organize my thoughts. There were so many questions I wanted to ask, but at the same time I didn't know how far I should go, due to the sensitive nature of his position.

After ten minutes of waiting, a handsome white man I assumed was Detective Jones, walked into the waiting room. "Vanessa Jackson?" he announced to no one in particular.

"That's me," I said, standing with my hand extended to shake his hand. "Thank you for meeting with me on such short notice."

"It's no problem. Why don't we step into my office?"

As I followed him down the hall, I could see why Dawn had been so attracted to him. Everything about him commanded attention and respect. His body was muscularly chiseled, with broad shoulders, and a tapered waist that displayed his clothes oh-so nicely. His posture was perfect, his hair closely faded, with an impeccably trimmed goatee to add an air of professionalism, and a nine-millimeter magnum neatly tucked into his gun hostler to complete the look that said "try me if you want to".

Once we were in his office, he offered me a seat before settling in behind his desk. With his fingers templed beneath his chin, he proceeded to silently size me up. After a long moment, he centered his blue eyes on my brown ones and sat back in his chair expectantly. "So what can I do for you, Ms. Jackson?"

"Detective Jones…"

"Please, call me Chris."

"Ok, Chris," I said placing my recorder on his desk, "I had a chance to interview Dawn Langston in depth about her life leading up to her crime. Obviously you were very close to her during the time of her arrest, and I just wanted to ask you a couple of questions about your perspective on the matter."

"Ok," he said warily.

"As one of the investigating officers on the scene of the Ross Styler murder case and for the Carmen Langston case, how did those experiences differ for you? I mean how did you feel when you saw Ross Styler's dead body, after knowing what he had done to Dawn's sister?"

He looked thoughtfully at me for a moment and then shook his head. "Ms. Jackson, I doubt I can answer that question on the record," he said, nodding his head toward the tape recorder I had laid on his desk. "But off the record, that might be an entirely different story."

I hit stop and slid the recorder over to his side of the desk so he could see that it was turned off. "Ok, off the record."

"Off the record, what was done to Carmen Langston was a tragedy to say the least. She was a kid and she had a very bright future ahead of her. I assume that you've seen her case file?" I nodded my head in agreement. "So you know what he did to her."

"As far as what I think about what she did to him," he went on to say, "honestly...I don't think it would be a bad idea to subject murderers to the same types of horror they put their victims through. If you shoot somebody and you get convicted then you should be shot, so on and so forth. But, I can't say that I think it's ok for people to take the law into their own hands.

Even though I understand what she did and why she did it, I can't condone it. I have to believe in the justice system, or else I wouldn't be able to come here and do my job everyday, Ms. Jackson."

I allowed what he had just said to sink in, while working up the nerve to ask the next question. "Were you really going to risk it all to keep her out of prison?" I blurted out.

He sighed heavily and then smiled to himself, as if lost in a memory. After a long pause he looked me in the eye and said, "In a heartbeat. I would have done anything to keep her out here...with me."

The sincerity of his words and the look on his face caused a lump to form in my throat. The love he felt for Dawn Langston was written all over his face, and it touched me to the depth of my soul. I will never forget that look for as long as I live.

"Thank you, Detective. I really appreciate you taking the time to speak with me." I excused myself and left the precinct without looking back. I had gotten what I came for and now I could finish my story.

Epilogue

I finished my story on Dawn Langston and it ran in the very next issue of the Women's Lib Magazine. That story stirred up so much controversy that it became the highest selling issue in the history of the magazine.

Dawn wrote me sometime later to let me know that she had finally found it in her heart to let go of the hatred she felt for Ross Styler. In letting go of that hate, she was finally able to forgive him and herself, and find the courage to ask God for forgiveness. She had even begun to write to the court of appeals to try to get her sentence reduced. She also informed me that Chris was still in her corner, as were her parents.

Her letter ended by thanking me for listening and asking me to keep her lifted up in prayer, so that she could find the strength to continue growing in the Lord. I was so moved by her sentiments that I was bawling by the time I reached the end of the letter.

Me, on the other hand, I decided after I handed that story in for editing that I was through being "the voice"…at least for a little while. Marion Hayes had opened my eyes to the fact that not everyone who went to prison was a bad person, and it is not for us to judge others based on our perceptions. Because sometimes, it only takes one cataclysmic event to send even the sanest individual over the edge.

Timberlynn Crawford had showed me that matters of the heart are never predictable and that love is not a game that should be played recklessly. And finally, Dawn Langston showed me that darkness lurks in the heart of the best of men, and given the proper time and circumstances we are all capable of doing the unimaginable.

Even though I had enjoyed tremendous success as "the voice" of incarcerated women, this assignment was to be my last. The Prison Chronicles would be laid to rest...

Be sure to check out these books by Janaya Black:
The Prison Chronicles Series
The Breaking Point

As Told By the Other Woman

Beautiful Rage: The Break of Dawn

Visit your local bookstore or order online at
www.black-smithenterprises.com

You may also view short film projects by Janaya Black
by visiting www.youtube.com/jblack317

Distributors:

Black and Nobel Books
1411 Erie Avenue
Philadelphia, PA 19140
215-965-1559

A&B Distributors
1000 Atlantic Ave
Brooklyn, NY 11217
718-783-7808

Lightning Source
1246 Heil Quaker Blvd
LaVergne, TN 37086
615-213-4491